The Captive

The Captive

SCOTT O'DELL

HOUGHTON MIFFLIN COMPANY BOSTON

Library of Congress Cataloging in Publication Data

O'Dell, Scott, 1903-
  The captive.

  SUMMARY: As part of a Spanish expedition to the
New World, a Jesuit seminarian witnesses the enslavement
and exploitation of the Mayas and his own seduction by
greed and ambition.
  [1.   Mexico – History – Conquest, 1519-1540 – Fiction.
2.   Mayas – Fiction.   3.   Indians of Mexico – Fiction]
I.   Title.
PZ7.0237Cap   [Fic]   79-15809
ISBN 0-395-27811-2

VB   20   19   18   17   16   15   14   13   12   11

Author's Note

This story is based on the legend of the Mayan god Kukulcán, who mysteriously appeared out of the north
some time around the sixth century. He was not born a
deity, it seems; he was a humble young man who, because of his compassionate nature, became a god.

Kukulcán lived among the Maya in what is now
southeastern Mexico until about the ninth century,
which was the flowering time of the culture. Grieving
over a misdeed, he disappeared into the east, saying, "I
leave you now but I shall come again. I shall come from
the east. You will find me in the body of a young man,
much younger than I, a tall youth with golden hair."

Among the Aztecs, Kukulcán was known as the god
Quetzalcoatl. When fair-haired Cortez marched upon
Mexico, the Aztec emperor, Moctezuma, thought that
the Spanish conquistador was the returning god. He
therefore delayed his defenses, received Cortez as Quetzalcoatl, and, in consequence, lost his kingdom.

Each chapter of *The Captive* is headed with a Mayan
number. Because the Maya had invented the zero, they
could add, subtract, multiply, and divide faster and far

more accurately than the Egyptians, the Greeks, or the Romans, who lacked a zero. The Maya used only three symbols: the dot, which stood for one; the bar, which stood for five; and the mollusk shell, which stood for zero. They combined these symbols in a twenty-base system (the numbers of fingers and toes; we use a ten-base system, the numbers of fingers only).

Mayan numbers read from top to bottom instead of from left to right. By combining dots and bars, the Maya could count up to nineteen before they had to jump to the next row. Each row could consist of up to four lines of symbols, as in the sign for nineteen. Each row had twenty times the value of the row beneath it. Our system of numbering, reading from the right, marks units, tens, hundreds, thousands. The Mayan system, reading from the bottom, marks units, twenties, four hundreds, and eight thousands.

The Captive is the first part of a story to be called *City of the Seven Serpents.*

—The Author

The Captive

●

By the cock that crew for our holy apostle St. Peter, by the bronze horse of Toledo and the six bishops of Valladolid, I swear that all I put down here is the truth. There is nothing else but the truth in this fateful story.

On an April morning of bright skies, after days of gentle rain, I was rousted from dreams with the point of a Toledo blade. It was a friendly jab Don Luis gave me, but meaningful nonetheless.

"Father Medina," said Don Luis, "has broken two of his legs. Had he more than two, the good father would have broken them also."

"How?" I blurted out. "Where?"

"No matter how and where. The legs are broken and I need two more to take their place. Sturdy legs. Yours, Julián Escobar. I need them today."

Dazed, I sat up and rubbed my eyes.

"Why me?" I stammered. "There are others. Father Expoleta, for one."

"Father Expoleta is old and, like the old, very set in his thoughts."

"But, sir," I said.

"Everything is arranged."

"But, sir," I repeated, staggering into my woolen short clothes. "How can I take the place of Father Medina? He is a priest, while I am only a seminarian. I am

1

ignorant of God's ways. I have barely begun my studies."

"Your studies can continue in the New World. On the island of Buenaventura."

"But my teachers are here," I protested. "My books are here. My friends. My mother. The cathedral of Seville, where I was baptized. The village of Arroyo, where I was born and wish to serve God. All are here, sir."

"God resides everywhere. Not here alone, but in the New World also. Even among the savages, who have never heard of Him. Among them especially. It will be your privilege to bring them His love."

"Privilege?"

"Your duty as a Christian, I should say."

"Duty?"

"Yes, because you will have power over them. These dark people will stand in awe of you, tall and fair-haired as you are. Your voice will charm them, as well. And your words, though they do lean toward the Latinate, will cast a spell upon them."

"But the words I speak are Spanish."

"Words are words. It is the sound of words that alerts the mind and soothes the heart. Not so much the words themselves."

As I brushed my hair, glancing in the mirror that hung beside my bunk, I was astonished to see my open-mouthed face.

"Not to mention your talents as a musician," Don Luis said. "The gittern, which you play sweetly, like an archangel. Like Gabriel himself."

I began to quibble. "Gabriel does not play the gittern. He plays a horn."

"I see you standing there in the jungle, surrounded by savage hundreds."

From the tone of his voice, I think he did see me standing in the jungle surrounded by savages.

"I hear your voice. I hear the sweet notes of your gittern dropping like honey. You will save many souls. Hundreds, thousands, far more than you ever will save here."

I continued my quibbling, meanwhile summoning the courage to face him down. "I lack clothes for the expedition. Where do I get them?" I said.

"Use those of Father Medina, he of the two broken legs who fell into an open cesspool while walking along in broad daylight, reading. Reading causes many misfortunes."

"He is half my size."

"We are not going to a fiesta."

"But, sir, I am awkward on a horse."

"True enough. Therefore, like your beloved Saint Francis, you will walk."

"I become seasick," I said.

"How do you know? In all your sixteen years, you have never set foot upon the deck of a ship."

"Just standing on the shore and watching the waves come and go makes my stomach churn."

Don Luis squinted his eyes. It was his manner of smiling. He smiled easily. He could squint his eyes as he stuck a sword smack into your gizzard. Then he surprised me by touching my shoulder. Although he was only twenty-seven, it was a fatherly hand he laid upon me.

"You are so absorbed in your studies," he said, "I doubt you have heard about the island granted to me by my cousin."

"I have heard."

"Do you know that it is twenty leagues in length and a full nine leagues in width?"

I nodded. For the past ten months, since the day the grant was made, there had been much talk about it in our village. In the last month, since Don Luis bought the caravel *Santa Margarita,* the countryside talked of little else. And the people of Seville knew about it, too. Carts and mules loaded with dried peas, salted fish and beef, oatmeal, firkins of flour, brown biscuits, white biscuits, and casks of wine left the Arroyo farms every week and clattered through the streets on their way to the river dock.

"You know," Don Luis continued, "that the island of Buenaventura has thousands of hectares of rich land, where, it is said, anything will grow. You only need to drop a seed on the earth and jump out of the way. Also, trees filled with all kinds of fabulous fruit never served here in Spain."

I nodded.

"And gold. The Indians pluck it with their fingers from the common ground they tread upon."

"Yes, I have heard this. Likewise that these savages make necklaces of gold so heavy it takes a strong man to wear one."

"And bowls of gold they eat gruel from."

4

"You will be a rich man," I said, without envy. "Richer than you are now. You will rival the king in riches."

I walked to the door and looked out. It was a beautiful morning. A silvery mist lay over the new-plowed fields. Far off, the spires of Seville caught the first rays of the sun. Birds were singing. I turned around to face Don Luis.

He slipped his sword in its sheath. He smiled. "We leave Arroyo at noon," he said. "We sail from Seville tomorrow at dawn."

I was silent, summoning the courage to speak my mind. It was not easy. Don Luis was a young man accustomed to being obeyed. He had done much for me. When my father had fallen mortally ill, he had forgiven my mother the family debts. Though she was in poor health and could work but little, he kept her on as a servant in his household. It was he who had made it possible for me to attend the seminary of St. Jude.

"I am honored that you wish me to go to the New World, but my ties are here," I said, repeating myself. "My companions, my school, and the people I hope to serve someday."

Don Luis smiled. "The village of Arroyo," he said, "which you wish to serve, possesses one hundred and ninety-two inhabitants. Added to this number are the one hundred and seven who work for me, making a total of two hundred and ninety-nine. In New Spain, on the island of Buenaventura, according to what I am told, there are more than two thousand Indians. These are savages who have never heard of God. Who are

5

fated to die without ever knowing Him." A very devout Christian, Don Luis paused to cross himself. "The people of our village need you," he went on, "but the savages of Buenaventura need you more. It is clear to me where your duty lies."

"But I'm not a priest. I still have two years of study."

"You can continue your studies in New Spain. The Bishop of Burgos is my close friend. It was through his influence that I was granted the *encomienda*. He will arrange this through the church in Hispaniola. What is more, once he takes you under his wing, once you have established yourself as a powerful saver of souls, opportunities you never dreamed of will come your way. You will not be stuck in the village of Arroyo for the rest of your life — baptizing babies, marrying the young, burying the old. This I promise you: one day you yourself will become a bishop. As powerful as the Bishop of Burgos."

Looking back now, years after that spring morning, I realize it was then, at the very moment when Don Luis spoke these words and I clearly saw before me a world of service I had never dreamed of before, that I made my decision.

"Again, may I remind you," said Don Luis, "we leave here at noon. We sail from Seville at dawn."

"Are you certain," I said, "that I will have a chance to pursue my studies there on the island?"

"Certain," said Don Luis. "Do not trouble yourself. Come, a new world beckons. You were never meant to be a village priest."

I watched as he turned away and crossed the courtyard, walking stiffly, as if he were marching to a drum. On his long bony face was the arrogance of a young nobleman who felt that the waiting world was a toothsome peach to be plucked.

He was not tall, but his feathered hat and the extra lifts he wore on his boots gave the impression of height. He looked like one of the court dandies, but he was not. He was a man of unusual courage. As an instance, he once made a wager with King Ferdinand, his cousin, that he could swim the Guadalquivir, not in summer, mind you, at a time when the river runs shallow, but in the midst of a spring torrent.

He swam the river, all right, but he was pulled out on the far bank, a half league from where he started, more dead than alive. Once again I saw him, on a dare, leap astride the neck of a young bull and ride the beast, holding to its horns, until blood spurted from his ears.

He was a fit match for the dangers of the New World, which I had heard about many times—for its wild animals, its deadly insects and fatal fevers, vipers that killed with a single bite, its fierce storms that could wreck a dozen ships and drown a thousand men, its savage Indians who shot poisonous arrows and lived upon human flesh. But would I, an untried village youth, be a match for this strange new world that lay far across the ocean sea?

I took down the three-stringed gittern and wrapped it carefully in the folds of my cloak. With it I placed my Bible and a small parcel of books. I had little else to carry.

● ●

We rode out of the courtyard at noon. Beyond the spires of Seville, the winding Guadalquivir glittered. A drum beat. Someone blew a horn. The flag-bearer held the pennon aloft, three Spanish lancers in pursuit of a band of fleeing Moors.

We were a small army marching forth. Don Luis rode behind the flag-bearer, astride Bravo, a black stallion with a single white star on its forehead. He was followed by six musketeers, six bowmen, four cannoneers, eight soldiers, all on mules, and five horses. Then came his interpreter and servant, Esteban, a slave from the New World whom Don Luis had bought from a trader two years before, and Juan Pacheco, his barber, surgeon, and astrologer, riding a dappled mare.

On foot, carrying my sandals because I owned only one pair, trailed by two gray mastiffs, I brought up the rear. I carried the bundle of small clothes and a parcel of books on my back, the gittern and the Holy Bible in my hands. My mother's tearful blessings rang in my ears. My heart beat loud against my ribs. Not knowing whether to weep or shout with joy, I commended myself to God.

Our little army passed through the iron gates and down the winding road. When we reached the city, storekeepers came out to cheer us on. Some shouted advice. Women waved handkerchiefs. Urchins ran along beside the cavalcade, pretending that they too were sailing for the New World.

By midafternoon we reached the caravel, moored at the river's bank a stone's throw from the watchtower, and, to the squealing of fifes, gaily filed aboard. But no sooner were we settled and the livestock bedded down than an argument arose between Don Luis and Captain Roa.

Three other caravels moored nearby, which belonged to the Duke of Salamanca, were making ready to sail for Hispaniola within the week. Captain Roa advised Don Luis to wait and join them, since it would be safer, he said, than if we sailed alone.

Don Luis, however, was eager to depart, the stars being in favorable conjunction, according to Pacheco. Furthermore, he disliked the Duke of Salamanca, a distant cousin. Since Don Luis owned the caravel and had financed the expedition, he could do what he wished. The argument was brief, despite the fact that Captain Roa was an experienced seaman, having sailed with Columbus on the Admiral's third voyage.

At sunrise, *Santa Margarita* left on an April freshet and swiftly made the open sea. Before she was out of sight of the river mouth, I fell sick and remained in that condition until we reached Grand Canary, seven days later. By this time the ship's routine had been well established — the various stints handed out and the watches set.

At sunrise on the first day that I was again on my feet, I was sent to the sterncastle, and Captain Roa introduced me to the *reloj de arena,* a sand clock. I was instructed to turn it as soon as the sand ran from the upper to the lower section. This measured exactly thirty minutes, a figure I entered in the log. The captain cautioned me not to daydream or to read the books which I carried around with me, for the ship's direction and the knowledge of where it was on the vast ocean sea depended upon accurate time.

After giving the sand clock eight turns, thus spanning the four hours of the first watch, and handing it over to the young man who followed me, I was sent to the hold, there to help feed and water the horses and mules. This took me until past noon, when I was allowed to scavenge for something to eat—a handful of olives, a clove of garlic, a few sardines, and a biscuit—since the only cook aboard cooked solely for Don Luis and Captain Roa.

The rest of the afternoon I was set to work splicing rope until my fingers bled. After supper, which was a matter of grabbing what I could, I was free to find a quiet place to settle down for the night.

The caravel was of average dimensions—twenty-seven strides from stern to bow and seven long strides in width. Much like Columbus' *Santa María* in appearance and, like her, carrying three masts, but with lookouts on two of them. The galley was located amidships and ran from port to starboard. She was painted black, with gold carvings on her bow and around the stern window.

To save space for cargo, the *Santa Margarita* was not outfitted with bunks nor hammocks. Except for Don

Luis and Captain Roa, each man fended for himself, finding a soft plank somewhere on deck or below, if he was lucky.

This, my first official day at sea, left me barely able to walk. As I located a place to lie down between two cannoneers and was settling myself to rest, Don Luis sent for me. He and Captain Roa were just beginning their supper as I entered the cabin.

"*Qué pasa?* What goes?" Don Luis said to me, but did not wait for an answer. "I asked Captain Roa to lead you a merry pace. You have survived, I see."

"Barely enough," I said.

"Now you know what it is to work aboard a caravel. Something you have not known heretofore. Tomorrow I will give you tasks more to your liking." And he went on to outline my new duties.

At dawn, in accordance with his wishes, I went to the sterncastle and there, from this high vantage point, in a loud voice so that all could hear, I sang out:

> Blessed be the light of day
> and the Holy Cross, we say;
> and the Lord of Veritie
> and the Holy Trinity.
> Blessed be the immortal soul
> and the Lord who keeps it whole,
> Blessed be the light of day
> and He who sends the night away.

The rest of the day was my own, to read, to think, to dream. Until sundown, when I again mounted to the sterncastle and this time sang the beautiful Salve Regina, in the best voice I could summon. Then I took up my gittern and went below, where Don Luis and Captain Roa were dining at a table set with white linen and silver.

Don Luis glanced at the gittern. "You anticipate my wishes."

On the contrary, I had not anticipated his wishes. The gittern was tucked beneath my arm because I could find no other place to put it. Like the rest of my companions, I had a parcel of deck to bed upon, where anything lying around would be stepped upon.

"Play!" Don Luis commanded me. "Nothing from the seminary. Something pleasant. Peñalosa?"

"Yes, sir."

"A song?"

"Yes, sir."

Don Luis turned to the captain. "Julián has much talent. He has taken many lessons."

While he went on to describe my musical gifts, I settled myself in a corner of the cabin, finding bare room to pluck the gittern, and began to play. I played throughout the long meal, which consisted of excellent fare—a flagon of red wine, such things as spitted fowl and venison.

The meal at an end, I was rewarded by a generous helping, which I ate upon the deck, alone in the moonlight, gazing at the dark outlines of the island.

Trouble, which had begun between the two men in Seville, broke out again while we were making ready to leave Grand Canary. Captain Roa argued that we should follow the same course Columbus had taken on his last voyage, some fourteen years before. On the contrary, Don Luis thought we should follow a more northerly course, based upon a recent chart—one made by Miguel Peña within the last few months—which he had studied at length.

Since Don Luis owned the *Santa Margarita* and had provisioned her and hired the crew and Captain Roa himself, it gave him the right, he was convinced, to run the ship. Small matter that he had never been to sea nor knew more than he had read in books and portolans.

We were scarcely out of the harbor, on the course he had selected, than we ran into a calm that lasted three days and three nights. When the wind did blow again, it barely filled the smallest sails. Another five days of these calm airs went by, with the result that, in two weeks of sailing, we had logged less than eighty Roman miles.

At this time Captain Roa became worried about the state of our water casks. He spoke his fears at the evening meal.

"By my reckoning," he said, "we need four weeks of good winds and fair weather until we can hope to make a landfall. Before that time we will run dangerously low on water. It is the mules that consume the water."

It was true about the mules. They drank more than all the men aboard.

"What do you wish to do," Don Luis said, "—toss them overboard?"

"No," the captain answered. "But it would be wise to double back to Grand Canary, refill our casks, and purchase more. A dozen casks, if possible."

"And lose time. Days. A week," Don Luis said. He

looked at me. "Julián, I put you in charge of the casks. See that the crew gets half-rations of water. The same for our men. You have good powers of persuasion."

Captain Roa shook his head. "It will cause trouble. Not with your men, but with the crew. All are jailbirds. Within an hour they will be at our throats."

Jailbirds they were, fresh from Seville's stone prison, men who had taken advantage of the royal edict that offered pardons to all who enlisted for a voyage to the New World. Their leader was Baltasar Guzmán. Señor Guzmán had a round head with close-cropped hair. A thin white scar ran from the corner of his mouth to his right ear, which was adorned with a gold ring. He looked as if he had been hacked from a tree trunk. With his iron fists he kept the men in line.

As I gathered up my supper and went on deck to eat it, my appetite quailed at the prospect of facing the cutthroat crew with the news that their rations of water had been reduced by half. But as events turned out, I had no need to face them.

• • •

The next morning, shortly before sunrise, we suddenly came upon what appeared to be a rocky pinnacle. It lay directly in our path, some quarter of a league off our starboard bow, shrouded in morning mist. But as we drew close upon it, our lookout reported it to be a two-masted, square-rigged carrack drifting slowly eastward under two slack sails.

Our spirits were greatly lifted at the sight, for it was the first vessel we had seen since leaving Spain. Wild cheers went up from the crew, and at once Captain Roa called through his speaking tube a long *hola*.

There was no answer. He hailed the drifting carrack three times, but not a sound came back to us. Nor could we see a soul anywhere upon her battered and salt-encrusted decks or in her rigging. I noted her name, *Santa Cecilia,* in faded gilt across her sterncastle.

We were barely a ship's length from the carrack when Captain Roa said, "There is a look about her that I do not like. There may have been a mutiny aboard. The mutineers can be hiding below deck."

As we moved away, Don Luis took charge and ordered the helmsman to circle back and come upon the carrack from our port side, where we had three cannon in position to fire a volley of round shot.

"I will take a few men and board her when we come

15

around," Don Luis said. "She seems seaworthy enough."

"Her sails are in tatters," replied Captain Roa. "Her masts are badly sprung. My advice is to stand off and give her a shot or two. She is not worth the risk of an ambush."

"That risk I will take," Don Luis said, drawing his sword. "We may have a prize in our grasp."

At the last moment, as we came broadside and were moving away, one of the crew tossed a boarding hook over the *Santa Cecilia*'s rail. The two ships bumped and then settled side to side. Don Luis leaped aboard, shouting, "Santiago!" His six musketeers, repeating the cry, followed hard on his heels.

I could see nothing over the high bulwarks. There was the sound of scurrying boots, of voices, a deep silence, then Esteban's name shouted by Don Luis, then my name, and the command *"Venga!"*

The first thing that met my eyes as I scrambled over the bulwark and set my feet upon the deck of the *Santa Cecilia* was the kneeling figure of Don Luis. (The six musketeers had disappeared, apparently down a ladder that led into the hold.) He was kneeling beside an old man, an Indian with sunken cheeks and lips that were bleeding, whose tongue as he opened his mouth to speak was swollen and black.

I thought first of finding water; then I saw that the cask the Indian leaned against was full and that he had already drunk from it. His voice was coming from a far-off part of his body, a thin croak like that of some forest animal. I took his hand in mine. It was like a bundle of

16

dry sticks, only wet with blood that did not have the look of blood but more that of thick, dark syrup.

Don Luis called Esteban, the slave, to his side and asked him to interpret what the old man was saying. Esteban put his ear close, as the Indian rocked his gaunt head slowly back and forth, and tried to find Spanish words for what he heard from the shriveled lips.

It appeared that the *Santa Cecilia* had sailed from an island near Hispaniola in the New World, carrying many slaves and commanded by a Spanish captain. This was some time in the past. It could have been two months ago or six; Esteban was not sure. The slaves mutinied and killed the captain and all the members of his Spanish crew.

The slaves tried to run the ship but failed. For this reason they wandered over the sea for a long time, swept by contrary winds. Water they had in plenty from frequent rains, but food ran low. They ate the leather chafings on the masts. They ate the dust the rats left. They ate the rats. From what the old slave said, they ate each other. Then some sort of plague struck them, and their limbs turned black and gangrenous. Their gums grew over their teeth.

I called to one of the crew, and he brought a cup of leftover soup. I held it to the Indian's lips, but he turned his head away.

Don Luis stood up and together with Captain Roa went aft to inspect the carrack's sterncastle. At that moment the musketeers climbed out of the hold and stood still at the top of the ladder, their faces white as chalk.

A sudden breeze started up, and with it, from the

17

bowels of the ship, came a stench that buckled my legs. One of the men pointed below, two quick thrusts of his hand.

Thinking that someone was in need, I clambered down the ladder into the dimly lit hold. What I saw I cannot describe. If I could describe what I saw, I would refrain rather than to relive it here.

Suffice it to say that bodies were piled high against the sides of the ship. No one was alive. No one could be alive in that place. The body of a long-haired Indian that I stepped over when I came down the ladder I stepped over again as I left. The soles of the man's feet had been gnawed away by rats, which were scurrying here and there.

We moved the old Indian to our ship and tried to get him to eat. He refused everything we offered, continuing to babble about the mutiny, how fortunate it was that he alone of all the crew had been spared. He died shortly before sundown, and as he was dropped over the side, I commended him to God.

Meanwhile Don Luis, against the objections of Captain Roa, decided to lay claim to the *Santa Cecilia*. The crew spent the afternoon hauling her water casks aboard and securing a rope to the carrack's bow. There was talk of putting a helmsman aboard her, but it was finally decided to lash the rudder. Near dusk we set off with the slave ship in tow, moving westward in a freshening wind.

At supper, while I was playing a group of gay Andalusian songs, Don Luis said, "We will have the crew clean the ship in the morning, and ..."

"It will take more than a morning," Captain Roa broke in. "A week."

"We have an extra set of sails we can rig up."

"They'll not fit."

"We will make them fit," said Don Luis.

"What about a crew?" Captain Roa asked. "She will not sail herself."

"We take three from *Santa Margarita*'s crew, three musketeers, and three of my soldiers."

Captain Roa gave up the argument, as he had given up others before. With his sheath knife he cut himself a generous slice of mutton, put it in his mouth, and chewed thoughtfully for a while. "What plans for the *Santa Cecilia*, providing we are fortunate enough to get her into port somewhere? I noted that she is fitted out as a slaver. The hold is penned off. Slaves are as good as gold. And there are thousands among the islands."

"An inexhaustible supply, I hear," said Don Luis.

I was in the middle of a tune when these last words were said. I stopped playing. It was not the words themselves so much as the way they were spoken that froze my fingers to the strings. I remembered my talk with Don Luis the morning I reminded him that I was a seminarian, not a priest, and that it should be Father Expoleta who should go. He had cast my suggestion aside, saying that Expoleta was too old and set in his thoughts.

The suspicion came to me now, as I stood there silently holding the gittern, that his objection to the old priest was not a matter of age nor stubbornness. Expoleta was a leader in the fight against the use of Indian slaves on Spanish farms. He was a part of the same fight that Las Casas was waging in Seville, at court, and in Hispaniola. It was a fight that Don Luis, like all the rich landowners of Spain, bitterly opposed.

I finished the piece I was playing, while the two men went on about the profits to be made from slaves. I played without pleasure, questioning for the first time Don Luis' motives in choosing me for his expedition, instead of Father Expoleta. In a dark mood, I left the cabin and went aft to the caravel's sternpost.

The evening was clear with a quarter moon rising. The salt-encrusted carrack wallowed dimly in our wake. The rope that bound us together looked as fragile as a silver thread. By the stroke of a knife the *Santa Cecilia* and its ghastly cargo could be set adrift. The helmsman, though he had no view of what went on astern, would know by the feel of the rudder that the carrack was free. If for some reason he did not, a member of the watch certainly would.

And yet it might not be reported. The crew had grumbled when we picked up the carrack, thinking rightly that it would make the voyage longer. And Captain Roa himself had said that she wasn't worth the trouble. There was a good chance that Don Luis would not know until morning that the *Santa Cecilia* was drifting far astern, too far away to bother with.

For two years now in the village of Arroyo, some sixty Indian slaves had been working on our farms, most of them in vineyards and olive groves that belonged to Don Luis. Half were young men and half were women and children. There were no old people among them.

As soon as the Indians arrived in ox carts from the riverside at Seville, they were unloaded at our village church and baptized into the Christian faith. I was struck, as I watched this baptism, by their gentle ways, even though they must have been sad at leaving their island homes and bewildered by what they now saw around them.

Since then, they had become a morose lot; even in church their faces showed no signs of happiness. Some of them had died during the harsh winter just past, and of those who were left, many were unable to do a day's work, which did not please their owners, all of whom came to believe that the Indians were indolent by nature. Don Luis was of this belief and said that he preferred black slaves from Africa to those from the New World.

During this time, I became concerned with the preachings of Bartolomé de las Casas, who was born and raised near our village of Arroyo. Las Casas was a violent enemy of slavery. Once he came to our village and spoke out against it, using verses from Ecclesiasticus to shame the landowners who worked their slaves long, hard hours and paid them nothing:

"The bread of the needy is their life; he that defraudeth him thereof is a man of blood.

"He that taketh away his neighbour's living, slayeth him, and he that defraudeth the labourer of his hire is a bloodshedder."

His zeal was so inspiring that before he left I swore to him and to myself that I would do all in my power to help the slaves who worked our fields and vineyards.

And to speak out, whenever the chance came, against slavery itself. But the chance had never come to me in the village of Arroyo.

A following wind sprang up as I stood there, staring at the rope that bound the two ships together. The *Santa Cecilia,* because of its broader sterncastle, caught the wind, moved closer to us, and for a moment the rope hung slack.

I heard bare feet treading softly along the starboard rail before I saw a moving shape and in the moonlight the glint of a knife. The man was unaware that I stood not five paces from him. He grasped the slack rope and, pressing it against a stanchion, severed it with three hard thrusts of his knife.

As he turned away, moonlight outlined his face and I saw that it was Esteban, the slave. At the same moment, looking up, his gaze fell full upon me.

His first impulse was to use the knife, for he raised it and took a step in my direction. I spoke his name. The knife still upraised, he halted.

"What you have done," I said to him, speaking slowly so that he would understand me, "I would have done. Go, before you are caught here."

Without a word he turned and left me. As I stood there in the shadows, I took a last look at the carrack, fast disappearing in the moonlit sea. Aloud, I repeated the solemn vow I once had taken before Las Casas, and silently I again said it to myself.

● ● ● ●

The helmsman soon discovered that the towing rope had been cut and reported it to the officer of the watch, who for reasons of his own waited until dawn to report to Captain Roa. Pleased at being rid of the carrack, the captain waited until Don Luis came on deck an hour later before informing him of the *Santa Cecilia*'s loss.

"Turn about," Don Luis shouted. "We will go and search her out."

"She may have sunk by now," said the captain, taking pains to conceal his pleasure. "If not, she is far astern. No telling at what distance. Nor upon what course she sails."

"Turn about," said Don Luis.

"I remind you," Captain Roa replied, "that our water casks are still low. If we lose a day or two hunting the *Santa Cecilia* we will again be in trouble. Furthermore, it is my belief that should I give your order to the crew, they would not obey it."

"Then I shall lop off a head or two. Find the culprit and bring him here."

"It was not reported to me until dawn. Which means that officers and crew will protect the man who cut the rope."

Don Luis, who was not a fool, strode back and forth for a while, then disappeared into the sterncastle, where he stayed for the rest of the day. But when I appeared at supper with the gittern under my arm, he was in a good mood. After two cups of wine, he even agreed that it was a wise decision Captain Roa had made.

"Let us now ask for rain," he said, and the three of us knelt while I prayed, beseeching God to hear our supplications.

After five days, when water once more ran low, our prayers were answered. It came on to rain, a steady downpour that we caught in sails and sluiced into our casks. With the ten casks we had taken from the *Santa Cecilia* filled to the brims, the captain was now certain that our supply would last until we made a landfall.

Easterly winds remained steady and we made good progress, logging an average of one hundred and thirty Roman miles for each day of seven. On the seventh day, Captain Roa changed course and we followed a rule he had discovered somewhere in his travels: "Sail southward until the butter melts, then sail to the west."

But despite the fine weather and our steady progress westward, the crew began to grumble. We were now some twenty-seven days from the mouth of the Guadalquivir and eighteen days from Grand Canary. The time seemed longer to men who all their lives had trod the cobbled streets of Seville, never the deck of a bobbing caravel. There was no talk of coming to the end of the earth and falling off into a fiery chasm or coming upon monstrous sea animals that could consume a ship in one swallow. Columbus had dispelled these fears several years before. I think it was our encounter with the *Santa Cecilia* that unnerved them.

In any event, to quiet the crew before serious trouble arose, Captain Roa began to keep two separate logs. One was a record of the actual miles we covered each day, which he held secret from the crew. The other was a log that was given out only after it had been changed. Thus, on a day when we covered one hundred and thirty miles, Roa might add twenty and post our run as one hundred and fifty miles. He had learned this ruse from Columbus. It had worked for him and it worked now for Captain Roa.

Toward evening on the fourteenth day of good weather, still running with a brisk wind at our stern under sunny skies, the watch saw a gull-like bird of sooty mien circle the caravel and land high upon our mainmast. Whereupon the watch cheered and those who were sleeping roused themselves and all to a man danced upon the deck.

I watched them from the sterncastle, waiting until they quieted down and the barber had finished curling Don Luis' beard before I got ready to sing the Salve Regina.

"A childish lot," Don Luis said. "A feathered visitor makes them dance. Call the captain; I want a word with him."

Captain Roa explained that the bird was a *rabo de junco.* "They are often found near land. But sometimes not. Columbus spied such a bird and thought he was within twenty-five leagues of a landfall. Columbus was wrong."

"This is not the story you'll tell the crew," Don Luis said.

"No, I will say that it is a happy sign. But they already think this."

"Is it? Tell me, is the bird that sits there on its lofty perch an omen of good or of evil?"

"By my reckonings, should fair weather continue, we are three days' hard sailing from the island of Hispaniola."

In fine spirits, I sang and played, and everyone on the *Santa Margarita* joined in, even the cutthroat crew and Baltasar Guzmán.

Toward evening the next day we overtook a large sea-going canoe crowded with Indians. We moved up into the wind and sat dead in the water while the dugout, which was as long as our caravel, came up beside us, propelled by what must have been three dozen men using long colored paddles.

Looking down upon them, I was struck by their thick bodies, which were painted from head to toe in swirls and stripes of violent yellow. And by their heads, which were shaven clean on one side; on the other side coarse black hair hung to their shoulders. Esteban identified them as Caribs, a savage tribe feared by all the other Indians of the Spanish islands.

He pointed to five natives, lighter in hue than the Caribs, who lay bound hand and foot in the prow of the big canoe.

"Captives," he said. "Soon they will be roasted and eaten. The Caribs are cannibals."

Don Luis instructed him to invite the Carib chieftain aboard our ship.

The cacique was a fat, broad-faced Indian who was sitting regally under a grass canopy. He gathered himself together with the help of several of his retainers and started up the rope ladder, followed by a half-dozen of his naked retainers. Esteban, prompted by Don Luis,

27

held up his hand and commanded the cacique to halt and advance with only three of his servants.

The cacique brought gifts of fruit, varieties I had never seen before, and the three servants carried large gourds filled with painted objects. Don Luis examined the trinkets but, finding them made of base metal, shook his head and pointed to a gold ornament that the chieftain wore suspended from a gold chain around his neck. At the same time he held out a double handful of hawk's bells, lively little bells fashioned for horses to wear.

The cacique, who had a strong, unpleasant smell about him, shook his head and motioned toward a brass bombard that Captain Roa had set up on the maindeck, ready to fire should the Caribs decide to attack us. In turn Don Luis shook his head, and the two men stood staring at each other until Captain Roa produced a small copper pot.

This the chieftain seized and put it to his nose. We were told by Esteban that he was sniffing it to see if it was made of copper, since the Indians deemed copper more valuable than gold. He then handed over a small gold object that looked like two snakes twined together.

"Ask him," Captain Roa said to Esteban, "how close we are to land."

The cacique answered by pointing westward, telling Esteban that it was close. "A big island, very close."

"Ask him," said Don Luis, "where the gold in the necklace he wears about his neck comes from."

The cacique pointed westward again. It was another island, he told Esteban, far bigger than the first he had spoken of. And farther away; five days' journey away. But there we would find much gold, cities made of gold.

The cacique went on talking, making many gestures with his dimpled hands, but Esteban for some reason of his own did not translate what he said, other than to say that it was about the far-off golden cities.

There were more small trades, but being eager to make a landfall before dark descended, Captain Roa gave orders to hoist sail. The Indians trooped down the ladder and, hailing us with happy cries, disappeared under our stern.

A sailor, Juan Sosa, a native of Arroyo, was climbing the mainmast with three of the crew when he suddenly paused. At the same moment I heard a whisper, as if a breeze had sprung up, and a flight of arrows passed over my head. Clutching himself, Juan fell backward into the sea. A command went aft to the helmsman and we began to circle back toward our fallen comrade, but the savages reached him first. They pulled him from the sea and flung his body among the pile of bound captives. A round of musketry from our deck did them no harm apparently, for they fast disappeared.

Near dusk we came upon a large island, presumably the one the cacique had spoken of. Captain Roa could not find it on his chart and admitted, after Don Luis had pinned him down, that he did not know exactly where we were; probably near the Caribbean island of San Salvador, which he presumed we had passed in the night.

Don Luis promptly named it Isla Arroyo and asked me to call upon God to bless the island. Captain Roa marked it down on his chart, making the area somewhat larger than it seemed to be.

Isla Arroyo was heavily wooded, with tall trees growing right down to the shore and a curving bay tucked in behind a jutting, rugged promontory. As he stood looking at the calm water, Captain Roa said that when the stars came out, he'd take readings that would show him our location. No one, he said, except Christopher Columbus ever made accurate sightings from the deck of a bobbing caravel. And the great Admiral himself always trusted his instincts more than the sightings.

Evening light fell upon the placid bay, the strip of white sand that fringed it. Cries of "ashore, ashore" from soldiers and bowmen and crew rose in a chorus as the anchors went down. But Don Luis forbade the *lancha* to be put in the water, and when men began to strip, making ready to set off for the beach, he threatened them with the lash.

"We go tomorrow," he said. "In daylight, when we have taken precautions against an ambush. Remember that we are now in the land of savages. We're not at home on the quiet banks of the Guadalquivir."

Esteban, standing beside Don Luis, backed up his master's warning not by anything he said, but by the grim look on his face. I felt that even in daylight, with soldiers on guard, he would prefer to stay on the ship.

To be truthful, I felt somewhat that way myself. The sight of the Indian captives bound hand and foot and piled in the bottom of the Carib canoe was still with me. As was the sight of Juan Sosa, struck by a flight of arrows, falling from the mainmast into the sea. Before me now was a black jungle where anything might lurk.

The fear that grips the heart when you are in God's presence, be it in the quiet of the night or upon your knees in prayer, this I know. But it was the first time in my life that I had felt the twinge of physical fear, raised as I had been in a place where one day was much like the next. Once, in a boyhood fight with the village bully, who had large hairy fists, I had received a flattened nose (signs of which, incidentally, I bear to this day). But the altercation had come about so surprisingly and the blow was so sudden that I had no time at all to be fearful.

In the dusk, with a wan moon rising over a mysterious island, I didn't blame Esteban for his silence.

After supper that night Baltasar Guzmán fell to talking about the golden cities the Carib chieftain had mentioned to us. He had sailed with Captain Roa on the last voyage Columbus made, and during this time, when they anchored at a place the Admiral named Costa Rica, he had heard tales about these cities, or so he claimed, and about a golden man who was the emperor of a place far to the south of Costa Rica.

"This man," Guzmán said, "rules a large country that is very mountainous. It has a seacoast where large canoes come and go, but mostly it is a country of high peaks and deep valleys and rushing waters. There is gold everywhere in this land. Everywhere you go you will find gold."

Pacheco, the barber, broke in, "This country is how far away?"

"Far. Very far. My understanding is that it would take many months to arrive there. By sea, through mountains and jungles and rivers. A long time, Pacheco."

"But worth it," said the ship's carpenter, Maldonado.

"Yes," said Guzmán. "The houses have gold floors and walls of gold, those of the poor as well as the rich. The streets that lead to these houses are paved with gold, blocks so heavy that it requires four men to lift just one."

The men sat with their mouths ajar. The armorer said, "But the golden man? What of him?"

"From the stories I have heard," said Guzmán, "he is called Lope Luzir, which means Lord of Great Lords. He is a young man still unable to grow a beard but tall and handsome with blue eyes, which seems a singular occurrence since he is Indian by birth.

"This lord has many strange habits. He begins his day at dawn, when his attendants carry him on a golden litter to a small lake among the reeds. There he strips away his night clothing, and two priests cover him with sweet oils. Then two more priests come and from head to foot cover him, even his face, with gold dust.

"As dawn breaks, he stands there with his arms raised to the sun in prayer. Then he walks into the lake and his attendants wash the gold from his body and dress him. This happens every day of the year. It happened to his father and to his grandfather. The bottom of the lake, it's said, is paved with dust, gold dust lying deep as the golden lord is tall."

The crew was silent. I started another tune on the gittern and was told to stop. The men pressed Señor Guzmán for more details of this fabulous land, and he supplied them, talking out of what he had heard or his imagination until the moon rose high and the watch was changed.

Later on when night had fallen, small fires appeared along the beach. The sound of voices came to us faintly across the water. But in the morning the beach was deserted, and there was no sign of life anywhere.

Don Luis had the *lancha* lowered and went ashore with his eight soldiers and six bowmen, leaving the rest of us aboard. He was gone for an hour or more, and I could see him moving along the edge of the jungle, appearing and disappearing among the heavy brush and tall trees.

After an hour he came back to the caravel in a hurry, sent the crew ashore, cautioned the bowmen and musketeers to be on guard and, with me and Captain Roa in tow and a sack of hawk's bells, returned to the island.

He led us up the sandy beach a half league to the banks of a stream that flowed through a narrow opening into the sea. Beyond this opening, masked from the sea by a forest of mangroves, was a wide lagoon. There upon the still waters of the lagoon rode more than a hundred canoes of various sizes, painted in many bright colors and moored to colored stakes.

"Those who own the canoes are hiding, but where?" Don Luis said to Esteban.

"They watch from nearby," the slave replied.

"Call them," Don Luis said. "Say that we come to trade. We come in peace."

Cupping his hands, Esteban let out a piercing cry. It died away, unanswered. But presently a man with a gray beard, naked except for a circlet of shells around his waist, appeared at the edge of the clearing. He waved, and Esteban went forward to meet him. They talked for a time, mostly with their hands, while a silent group of young men came out of the shadowy forest and gathered around.

Esteban and the cacique, followed by his men, who carried short bows and a bundle of arrows, then came up to Don Luis. The cacique bowed and was about to drop to his knees when Don Luis put out his hand and gently stopped him. I noticed that at this moment his eyes took in with one swift glance the ornament the chieftain wore around his neck. It was a clump of gold, half as big as an apple, studded with small objects that looked like pearls.

Guzmán brought out a basket of trinkets and spread them on the ground in front of the cacique—green and blue beads, hawk's bells, holland shirts, and red caps.

In return, the cacique brought ten braces of fowl, maize cakes, prickly pears, and gourds filled with plums. Then Don Luis asked Esteban to translate his words and in his most commanding voice said to the chieftain and his servants:

"We have come to this beautiful island in the name of Our Lord Jesus Christ and our Royal King and Queen and of our advocate, St. Peter. We come in peace, with love in our hearts, to explain to you our holy faith."

Here Don Luis paused and had a small image brought forth of Our Lady with her Child in her arms. Then he explained to them that this image was a likeness of the Blessed Mary, who dwells in the high heavens and is the Mother of Our Lord.

The cacique listened carefully, his lips moving as Esteban translated, and when the speech was finished he bowed as if he understood everything and welcomed us to his island, which was called Tecoa. Beyond him, I noticed that many of his subjects — men, women, and children — had gathered and were shyly looking out at us through the underbrush.

Don Luis had a rude cross brought, two tree limbs held together with rawhide, and had it planted in front of the cacique and again asked Esteban to translate as he explained its true meaning.

"This is like the cross," he said, "upon which Our Lord Jesus Christ was fastened and put to death."

He told how afterward Our Lord was buried and how He rose from the dead. When Don Luis was finished he turned to me, asking that I bless the chieftain and his people. I replied that I could not, as a seminarian, bless anyone; only a priest could do that.

Don Luis smiled. "You look like a priest, with your gray gown and pious expression."

"I am not a priest."

"Priest or no priest, what does it matter? *No importa.* It's the spirit that counts."

"Spirit does count."

"Mumble, if you please. Say anything."

His words chilled me. "I will say what I wish and not as a priest."

It was the first time in our many years of friendship that I had stood my ground against him. Seeing that I meant to stand firm, he smiled and said, "Then sing. Sing the Salve Regina. Sing in your best voice, in your loudest and softest tones. Sing like a dove; sing like a lion. We will give the savages something to stir their hellish hearts."

For the first time I felt that he had only contempt for the Indians he yearned to save.

"Venga!" he said and pushed me forward a step.

Before I began to sing, I heard him ask Baltasar Guzmán if he thought that the objects the cacique wore on the gold ornament were pearls. And I heard Guzmán reply, "We shall find out."

The white objects in the chieftain's gold necklace were indeed pearls.

The Indians gathered oysters in the lagoon from rocks and the trunks of mangrove trees. It is said that these open during the night when feeding. Before they close at dawn, drops of dew fall upon the lips of the shells and thus in time pearls are formed. I do not know whether this is true or not, but I do know that the Indians were in the habit of harvesting the oysters for food and in them sometimes found pearls of great beauty, which they fashioned into ornaments.

On the day following our meeting with the cacique, Don Luis brought a sack of glass beads ashore and made a pact with him to trade it for a sack of pearls. The cacique called out all of his young men and set them to gathering oysters, which they brought by canoe to a central place at the head of the lagoon. There, they opened the shells, using knives that Guzmán furnished.

The young men took their time, however, talking and laughing, as was their wont. This displeased Don Luis, for he was eager to go in search of his island *encomienda,* which we had somehow missed and which Captain Roa, by his new calculations with the astrolabe, placed some hundred leagues south and presumably east of where we were now anchored.

To hasten matters, Don Luis brought ashore a chest of more holland shirts and persuaded the cacique, whose name, Esteban told us, was Ayo, to call upon all the women of the tribe, even the old, to help with the harvest.

The harvest went on for more than a week and produced two hundred and fifteen pearls, some as big as olives and many, according to Baltasar Guzmán, perfect in shape and orient.

One morning during this time, with the help of Ayo, the cacique, I managed to get the tribe together before work began. There were more than three hundred of them and they came, I am certain, because Ayo ordered them to. They also came because they had never seen a young man with long blond hair who sang in a deep voice and played a strange-looking, strange-sounding instrument. On the second morning and for several mornings thereafter about half the tribe appeared.

To these, using Esteban to translate my words, I told the story of Christ. I held up the image of Mary and explained to them that she was the Mother of Christ. I taught them to kneel and to repeat after me a simple prayer. I sent them off to work with a lively tune. In every way I knew, I did my best to win their trust.

I did win it. They were quiet and attentive as I spoke and while I sang and played. Many of them lingered after the little services to trade Indian words for Spanish or to touch my hand or simply to stand and look at me and shyly smile.

Yet I was filled with doubt, doubt that I would ever do more than win their trust. I was not a priest and

39

therefore could never hope to celebrate mass or conduct the rite of baptism or the rites for those who were dying.

Most of all, I doubted that I possessed the spirit or the patience to explain to these heathen people—who wore plugs in their noses and painted their bodies from head to foot, and worshiped hideous wooden images—to explain Christ's story and expect them to understand it.

And with these doubts the suspicion grew that Don Luis had brought me to New Spain not so much to spread the Christian faith as to use me. In his role of *encomendero*, owner of a vast and fertile island, whose riches he planned to harvest, with lordly power over its inhabitants, even of life and death, my presence could be of help. Whether I was successful in my mission to convert the Indians to the Christian faith was not as important to him as keeping them in good spirits. Friendly Indians, he reasoned, worked harder.

When the pearling showed signs of coming to an end, Don Luis and Guzmán decided to investigate the village, which lay far back in the jungle. It was built in this secret place, the cacique told us, to protect it from the marauding Caribs. But the two men thought otherwise.

"They have a storehouse of gold," Guzmán said. "Gold idols hidden away they don't want us to see."

Don Luis agreed, but he was polite about his request to see the village. He spoke softly to Ayo, smiling all the while. Guzmán, who thought that the Indians understood only strong words, said to the cacique, "See here, in friendship we come to your island in the name of our holy majesties and in the name of God on high, ruler of all. We are your guests and should be treated as guests and shown where you live."

It was a bright morning, with the sun already hot, though it was not much after daybreak. The sun glanced on Guzmán's sword as he stood facing the cacique.

The cacique said, "If I was a guest in your country— wherever it is and however great—I would not expect to go anywhere it pleased me."

Esteban had trouble translating these words, taking a long time at it. Guzmán paced up and down, with his hand on his sword, as if he were ready, indeed eager, to use it.

I was standing off by myself, in an effort not to seem a part of the argument, but was listening. I had decided on the first day to keep a distance from Don Luis and Guzmán, whom it was apparent the cacique mistrusted.

A small boy was tugging at my robe, holding up a red and yellow parrot he wished to barter. Ayo turned and motioned for Esteban and me to follow him.

Don Luis gave me a sign to go. Disappointed, Guzmán was silent.

The way was tortuous, crossing a rushing stream six times, skirting a deep chasm, snaking for a quarter of a league through a tunnel of underbrush where it was necessary to stoop as you moved along. I had the unworthy fear that I might not return.

The village was not impressive. It sat on a bank of the stream, a single row of brush and wattle huts thatched with palm leaves and hemmed in by towering trees. It looked as if the sun never shone upon them except at noontime. There were only a few Indians about, mostly old men and children. It was an unlikely place to store gold.

Sensing my disappointment, the cacique explained that his people spent the day in the forest or fishing in the sea or digging clams in the lagoon. The village itself they moved about, burning down the old huts when someone died, and building new ones in a different place. They were always on the alert for their enemies, the Caribs.

Near the far end of the row of huts, standing in a small clearing, I noticed what seemed to be a tall figure leaning against the trunk of a tree. As we drew nearer, however, I saw that it was a stone idol in the shape of a three-headed figure, with bright blue hair hanging to its shoulders. Its three mouths, which were agape, showed uneven rows of blood-red teeth.

As we approached, the cacique knelt and touched the earth with his forehead and spoke a word thrice over, which I took to be the idol's name. The name sounded like Motalapawn. Flowers and fruit lay at its feet.

I stopped in horror. My impulse was to seize a rock that lay close by and smash the idol's grinning faces, to strike the hands that were cupped together and held a small turtle with three heads. Instead, I stood stone still.

The cacique was watching, waiting for me to speak.

To this moment I had no clear idea of what Don Luis meant when he said that the Indians we would find in New Spain were savages who worshiped strange idols.

The idols I had pictured in my mind would have, if

not human forms, at least human characteristics. But this monstrous figure with its blood-red teeth belonged to a world I had never glimpsed.

Waiting for some word from me and not hearing it, Ayo bowed again to the ghastly idol, and led me away.

I studied him as he went down the trail that led to the lagoon. He walked as if he had reverence for the earth he trod upon, for the trees he passed and the running water. He stopped to pick a wildflower and place it in his hair. His people, as I had observed them in the few days I had been on the island, were much like him — gentle, courteous to each other, given to laughter whenever there was the least thing to laugh about.

How, then, did these happy people ever conceive this horrible god and fall down in worship before it? What would they ask of it? What could they ever receive?

As I went down the trail I swore to myself that I would destroy their hideous idol. Yet not by force. I would destroy it by revealing Christ's loving message to them. They would no longer live in bloody idolatry. Don Luis had talked of saving hundreds, thousands, of souls, so many that fame would lift me into a bishop's chair.

The thought had tempted me; indeed, it had set my feet upon this journey. The thought seemed selfish now. All I could see at this moment was the blue-haired, bloody-fanged figure standing silently in the jungle.

I did not intend to tell Don Luis about the idol, for he would go at once and destroy it, which certainly would lead to strife.

Don Luis was waiting at the lagoon. Beside him stood

43

Guzmán, with a fistful of pearls harvested during the day. They both looked hopefully at me.

Don Luis said, "Tell us what you saw."

"It's a small village," I said. "A row of huts along a stream."

"Gold?" Guzmán asked, turning the pearls over in his hand. "What of the gold?"

"I saw none."

"It could be hidden."

"I think that what they have, they wear."

"It comes from some place nearby," Don Luis said. "Five days' journey westward, the cacique said."

"We will find gold here on the island."

Don Luis took the pearls from Guzmán and began to examine them one by one. He said nothing about idols and, as I had planned, I said nothing.

As I walked away, Guzmán came up behind me and put a heavy arm on my shoulder.

"See here, Julián. Are you telling the truth about the village? It being only a row of *jacales,* huts, and so forth?"

"As I've said, señor, it is a poor village."

Guzmán stepped back and fixed me with a searching gaze. His eyes were set so deep in his head that I could not tell their color. But I saw among the folds of flesh that partly hid them a darkish glint.

"You're telling the truth?" he asked, speaking, as he seldom did, in a quiet voice.

"The truth," I replied quietly, though he greatly annoyed me, and moved away from him.

•••
___

Guzmán was not satisfied with my answer nor with what he had learned from the cacique. Certain that there was gold somewhere on the island, he went among the natives, asking questions, threatening them if they dared to lie.

He learned nothing at first, though most of the Indians wore gold necklaces and ear plugs. But on the day the pearling stopped and one of the cacique's sons came aboard the *Santa Margarita* to receive the tribe's share of the harvest, Guzmán confronted him below deck. What took place between them there in the dark hold no one knew, except that a scream was heard and shortly afterward the cacique's son came on deck, one of his hands cut and bloodied.

The next morning Guzmán disappeared up the stream that flowed into the lagoon. He came back that night with the news that he had discovered a gold pebble lying in a pool half a league up the stream.

Guzmán had worked in a quicksilver mine in Spain and had made, so Captain Roa said, a fortune in gold near Hispaniola, a fortune soon lost at tarok. Being experienced in mining, he knew that the gold pebbles came from nearby, since they were rough-edged and not smooth, which they would have been had they traveled any distance.

With two soldiers he set out to find the source of the gold shaped like pebbles. After two days of searching along the banks, he discovered a vein of pure metal, nearly the width of a hand, that ran back from the stream for more than thirty paces and at last lost itself in a rocky hill.

Guzmán reported the discovery to Don Luis, who spoke to Ayo and asked his permission to mine it. The cacique stood for a while, looking down at his toes and thinking. Then he said he wanted something in return. It happened at this moment that Bravo, the black stallion, who was tethered nearby, gave forth a powerful neigh.

The cacique looked up. "The horse," he said to Esteban, "the big horse I want for the gold."

Don Luis said to Esteban, "Tell the chieftain that the big horse he cannot have, since it was a birthday gift from my grandfather, who is now dead. Blessed be his sainted memory. But the chieftain can have any one of the other fine horses he wishes. And a saddle with silver on it."

"Besides the horse and the silver seat," the cacique said, "I wish one half of the gold."

"One half," Don Luis agreed.

The suddenness with which he agreed and the tone of his voice made me think he had no intention of giving the cacique so much as one *onza* of the gold.

"Who digs the gold?" the cacique asked.

Don Luis said, "You have many men who are young and strong and have little to do. They dig. Señor Guzmán here will tell them how to dig and where. He has had much experience with digging."

A gray gelding that had not survived the voyage well was given over to the cacique, and a saddle trimmed with silver, and a halter hung with hawk's bells.

Our horses had been a wild curiosity from the very beginning. At first the Indians stood off and looked at them from a distance, from behind a tree if one was handy. Gradually, a step at a time over days, they approached the horses and at last began to feed them. So the gift of the gelding was a big event, which they celebrated with drums and songs.

Guzmán got together a band of a dozen Indians that same afternoon and went upstream to start work on the gold reef. They carried iron mattocks, long-handled tools, each with a blade set at right angles to the shaft, and a keg of gunpowder.

They mined the vein of pure gold and blasted the rock that lay around it. This ore they carried in baskets down to the lagoon, where they piled it up, awaiting the completion of a rock crusher, a two-stone *arrastre*. By evening of the second day, when a mound of ore rose shoulder-high, Don Luis called all the workers together and gave them glass trinkets. He was greatly excited by the gold. The harvest of pearls was valuable, but the shining metal embedded in the yellow rock that lay piled up in front of him made his eyes dance.

When we had all gathered around him, he raised his sword and said, his voice quavering with emotion, his pale cheeks flushed with color, "Henceforth and forever more, I wish this island to be known as Isla del Oro." He turned to Captain Roa: "Rub out the old name and put the new name down on your chart just as I've spoken it."

"It would be better," said the captain, "if you were to confer with the governor before the new name is entered. The island may belong to someone else and have a different name."

"Put it down," said Don Luis.

That night while I was playing the gittern, rendering a tune that I thought was especially pretty, Don Luis told me to stop. Putting down the shank bone he had been sucking, he turned to Captain Roa.

"Captain, from what Guzmán says, we have a rich mine."

"He should know. He's seen many."

"How distant is Hispaniola," Don Luis asked, "now that you have made your celestial calculations?"

"Two hundred leagues or less."

"Is the *Santa Margarita* in shape to sail?"

"As much as she will ever be."

Don Luis picked up his shank bone and sucked on it for a moment. "We leave in the morning," he said. "I wish to talk to Governor Santacilla."

At dawn the two of them and a crew of eight set off for the island of Hispaniola, leaving for our protection some of Don Luis' men.

No sooner had Don Luis left the harbor than Guzmán set about increasing the yield of gold. He called the women of the tribe together, gave them bolts of silk cloth to share, and, with the help of the cacique, put them to work carrying baskets of ore to the lagoon. This freed men to work in the mine.

The yield increased, but Guzmán was not satisfied. Again with the help of Ayo, he divided the men into two bands, each laboring twelve hours. A steady stream of ore came down the trail on the backs of the women.

Five days after Don Luis left for Hispaniola, Guzmán had finished building an *arrastre*. Our animals were in poor condition from the hard voyage, so in their place Guzmán selected eight old men to turn the two flat stones that crushed the ore. Working in pairs for an hour at a time, pushing against the long wooden handle that turned the stones, they managed to keep up with the ore that the women brought down the trail.

After the ore was crushed, it was taken to the stream and washed. The gold, being heavy, sank to the bottom. Mostly in pebbles and flat pieces the size of coins, it was then stored in a shed that Guzmán had had built beside the lagoon. He posted night and day guards around the shed and in addition stationed our two mastiffs beside it. The Indians feared these big gray dogs, and rightly, for the beasts had been trained to attack and kill upon command.

Before Don Luis had been gone a week, the whole village was at work. Guzmán blasted the rock. The young men dug with mattocks and their hands. The women carried the ore to the lagoon. The old men turned the heavy stones of the *arrastre*. Everyone, whether lame or halt, had something to do. The shed overflowed with treasure.

My feeble efforts to bring these people Christ's message came to an end.

It had been difficult in the beginning, since I was ignorant of the language and needed to rely upon Esteban to translate what I said, to teach them things they had never dreamed of. It was now impossible. They knelt, after a long day of work, while I sang the Salve Regina. But then they rose and went off without a word.

There was nothing I could do about it. I couldn't expect help from Guzmán, who thought everything I did was not only a waste of time but also a hindrance to what he was doing, which was to mine as much ore as possible in the shortest time. He lived in fear that, before Don Luis returned, some questing Spaniard might sail into the harbor with a grant to the island. Or a band of adventurers might happen along and seize the shed filled with treasure.

I couldn't expect much help, if any, when Don Luis returned. Since the day of our arrival on Isla del Oro, he had grown more and more like the greedy Guzmán. His voyage to Hispaniola was no more than an effort to accumulate new lands and new Indians to work them. His ambition, I felt certain from hints he had let fall to Captain Roa, was to become the most powerful *encomendero* in New Spain.

Sixto Gonzales, the ship's gunner, stationed at the northern arm of the bay with instructions to report anything out of the ordinary, fired a musket shortly after dawn of a mist-shrouded morning.

It was now nine days since Don Luis had left for Hispaniola. My first thought when I heard the sound of the musket was that he had returned. I was at the lagoon talking to three boys, trading Spanish words for Indian. I started at a run for the bay, some half a league distant.

I broke out of the jungle as I came to the sea and ran along the beach to where Sixto Gonzales was perched on a flat rock. I peered seaward, looking for the sails of the *Santa Margarita.* I saw nothing except a small red canoe, which belonged to an old man who fished the bay every morning for sharks, whose skins his wife and daughters used to make sandals. He had hold of something and was being towed along at a good rate.

A moment after I sighted the old man, Sixto Gonzales fired the big bombard. I saw the shot fall into calm water northward of the cannon smoke. Beyond the fountain it raised, I saw a swarm of painted canoes.

A large canoe, manned by dozens of paddles, led the way. It was striped yellow and blue, in the same design, the same colors, I remembered from our encounter short weeks before.

Sixto Gonzales stood beside the cannon, a spyglass to his eye. He confirmed my suspicions.

"Caribs," he said. "The canoe that leads them has the Carib figurehead." He turned to his helper and gave instructions about loading the bombard. "A double charge, Porfirio. We will blow them into the deepest pit." He took hold of the lanyard, making ready to fire, and motioned me to shoulder the musket. "Do you comprehend its workings?"

"Not at all," I said. "I have never held one in my hands."

"You know one end from the other? Good. Now put the blunt end to your shoulder, your finger under the guard, lightly on the trigger, take a deep breath, and wait for orders, which I will give presently."

The iron ball, a large one, had struck in front of the Caribs. As the column of water rose across their bow and the cannon roared and echoed over the bay, the swarming canoes stopped dead in the water.

Meanwhile, the musket shot had alerted Señor Guzmán. He suddenly appeared on the beach, with four men fully armed. When Sixto Gonzales saw that there were no natives among them, he shouted down to Guzmán, "The Indians. Where are they?"

In disgust, Guzmán spat upon the sand. "Hiding," he shouted back. "All of them — men, women, and children. They hide."

"We do not need the natives," said Sixto Gonzales.

"No, but they would not hinder us," Guzmán replied. "Later I will try to rally them."

I stood looking at the two men, amazed at how calm

they were. A hundred savages and more paddled toward us, making ready to attack, and yet they acted as if they were on parade. In all the days I lived in the New World, my amazement never ceased at the calm way the Spaniard faced danger and death.

Part of this bravery, the certain belief that, be the enemy one or one hundred, he still was equal to the challenge, came from a lust for treasure. The conquistador dreamed of slaves and gold. He talked of little else.

And another part of it came from an arrogance that a Spaniard like Don Luis drank in with his mother's milk. It never left him even in defeat, for he felt that he was doing God's work, at God's command, and that in the end God would not desert him.

To be truthful, I had been as arrogant as any. I, Julián Escobar, I too had lusted. I had lusted for souls, dreamed and talked of little else. The difference was that I seemed to lack the sure belief that Don Luis possessed.

The Caribs had recovered from their surprise at the cannon roar and the water spout, which I presumed they had difficulty explaining to themselves, being ignorant of both. They now had formed a single file, the big canoe in the lead, and were slowly rounding the promontory, watching the beach as they came.

Three of Señor Guzmán's guard, what Don Luis had left him, appeared on muleback, dragging a cannon and a sled stacked with shot. The cannon was placed in position and made ready to fire. Two bowmen and two musketeers stood ready behind them.

Paddling for a few moments, then coasting, the Caribs skirted the beach within range, but Guzmán held his fire.

"Wait until they make up their minds," he said to Sixto Gonzales. "By now they have made out that we are Spaniards. This is giving them thought."

"As well it might," Sixto answered.

The Caribs had reached the promontory that formed the southern boundary of the bay and were returning, now at a more rapid pace and closer to the beach.

The morning was hot and quiet. I could hear the savages jabbering among themselves. They began to chant, a jumble of words in a high, excited pitch. As the canoes reached the northern limits of the bay and made a wide turn that brought them closer to us, I heard a familiar voice speaking. It belonged to the fat Carib chieftain I had seen once before. As his words came clearly across the quiet water, Esteban translated them as soon as they were spoken.

"Dogs," the cacique said, "we come to eat your arms and legs and fingers. We shall consume your flesh with sweet mango sauce."

A chorus of insults went up from his followers. Guzmán answered by raising his hand to Sixto Gonzales. The two brass cannon roared at once. The shots struck in the midst of the swarming canoes. One sent up a spout and seemingly did no harm, but the other lifted the big canoe into the air and turned it over, end for end. At the same time, our musket fire poured down upon those struggling in the water, among them the fat cacique.

A flight of fire arrows immediately fell upon the

promontory, wounding the two bowmen and setting ablaze a keg of powder.

No longer were the Caribs shouting insults. Their big canoe was sinking fast. Those in the water clambered into other canoes; then the whole fleet moved swiftly seaward. Behind them, a dozen or more bodies floated on the tide.

Sixto Gonzales wanted to send a parting shot after them, but Guzmán told him to hold his fire. "If I know them, they have not gone," he said. "They will regroup, lick their wounds, and return."

As he spoke, the Caribs made a quick turn, all the canoes at once, and headed for the northern arm of the bay, where the jungle reached down to the sea.

"They'll come back," Guzmán said. "We are at a disadvantage now, with our two bowmen wounded. And we can't count upon Don Luis arriving. We need to choose a good place to defend ourselves."

He was fearful that the Caribs would go ashore somewhere and then creep back through the jungle and fall upon us from the rear. He also feared that on their way they might happen upon the gold he had stored away. We therefore left our place, with the wounded bowmen on the sled, the mules dragging the cannon, and returned to the lagoon. There, Guzmán grouped us around the shed, seven of us and the two big dogs. I was still clutching the musket, about which I knew little.

The *arrastre* was silent. There were no Indians in sight. Thinking to rally them, Guzmán fired one of the cannon. The echoes had scarcely died away when Ayo appeared out of the thicket of thorn bushes, followed by two of his retainers.

"We are outnumbered," Señor Guzmán said to him. "We can defeat the Caribs, but it will take longer to do so unless you lend us a hand."

"We trust that you are victorious," the cacique replied, "but my people are few. Once there were many. I have lost many of my people."

"Give me two dozen young men, armed with spears, and I will exterminate your enemy. You'll not need fear them again for many years."

"I cannot give you two dozen men."

"Half that number."

"None," said the cacique. "There is no will among my people to fight."

Señor Guzmán stared at the cacique in disbelief. "You would rather die than fight?"

"We have learned to survive by not fighting."

The sun poured down. Guzmán wiped the sweat from his brow and grabbed the musket from my hand.

"You will now learn to survive by fighting," he said.

"Your retainers, I see, are armed. I will arm you. Here, Sixto, give him your sword."

Sixto unbuckled his weapon and thrust it toward the chieftain. Ayo stepped back and wouldn't take the sword.

Guzmán ran his tongue over his lips. "We fight in your behalf," he said. "I invite you to help us in this fight."

"It is not our fight," Ayo said. "The Caribs did not come for us. They are tired of our flesh. They have told us so. It is your flesh they hunger for."

"Grasp the sword you are offered," Guzmán commanded, "and join us in the fight."

Ayo glanced at the sword Sixto held out to him. He hesitated, as if he considered taking it. In the trees close by a child was crying. For a moment he seemed to listen to the sound; then he stepped back, refusing the sword, and turned away.

Guzmán strode to the shed where the two big mastiffs were tethered, untied one of them, and brought it back, straining on the leash.

Ayo was walking away, up the path he had come by.

In a calm voice Guzmán said, "Halt. Go no farther."

The cacique walked on, his two retainers on either side. Whether he understood the command or even heard it, I cannot say.

Guzmán gave the order again. This time he shouted.

The cacique was nearing the jungle when Guzmán unleashed the mastiff. The dog bounded up the path in great leaps, as if it were chasing a rabbit. I don't think Ayo heard it coming, for the dog moved without a sound. Not until he had reached the thickets at the edge of the jungle did the cacique turn, perhaps to say some last defiant word, and from the distance face Guzmán. The mastiff caught Ayo in the throat and bore him to the earth, shaking him like a bundle of sticks.

Guzmán called to the dog. It came leaping back and sat at his side, its bloody tongue hanging out.

When the chieftain's body was gathered up, shrill cries came from the jungle, followed as the day waned by a chorus of bitter lamentation.

My mission, I was aware, had come to an end. I would be blamed for Guzmán's brutal act. No preaching of mine nor stories nor songs would win back the Indians' trust. I had much to think about that night.

Two days after the death of the cacique Ayo, the *Santa Margarita* sailed in from Hispaniola. Don Luis came ashore as soon as the caravel dropped anchor, dressed in polished boots, a new red-lined cloak, and a leather hat with a long green feather. From his wide smile and jaunty walk I judged that he had been successful in his request for a grant to Isla del Oro. But such was not the case.

"We were too late by a month," he confessed. "A Señor Olivares, brother-in-law of the governor, is now outfitting a caravel in Hispaniola and will arrive here any day to take possession of the island."

"This means," said Guzmán, "that we lose no time moving the gold to the ship. And work all day and by torchlight to dig as much more as we can."

He then gave Don Luis his own bad news, an account of the Caribs' attack, the refusal of Ayo to help at a moment when his help was needed, why he had been compelled to kill Ayo, and how the whole village thereupon had fled into the jungle.

The three of us were walking toward the horses, which stood waiting on the beach. Don Luis stopped and threw up his hands.

"How do we mine gold without Indians?" he shouted.

"We find them and bring them back," said Guzmán.

"I've planned things out, pending your return. We need some of the *Santa Margarita*'s crew and all the soldiers. We should leave today."

"In what direction? Where did they flee, these runaways?"

"One didn't flee in time. I have this one bound to a tree. Already I have some information."

Guzmán paused to give his fist a meaningful turn. "Before the hour is gone I'll extract more."

I was silent through all of this, as I had been at Ayo's needless death. I knew that anything I said to Guzmán would be ignored. I felt it wiser to wait until I was alone with Don Luis and had a chance of being heard, at least to vent my anger, whatever the outcome. The chance came in a few moments.

As Guzmán strode off to wring more information from the Indian he had bound to a tree, I spoke to Don Luis, saying first that I was glad he had returned. I told him I was outraged at the murder of my friend Ayo. I told him that Guzmán had done things in his absence that only a brutal man would do.

"My efforts to win over the Indians to our Christian faith," I said, "he has undone. He has worked them so hard, night and day, that they no longer have the strength or even the desire to hear my words. I've lost all that I gained when you were here."

"Yes, the Indians work hard, but don't forget the cost of the caravel *Santa Margarita*. More than forty thousand pesos. Provisions, five thousand. Not to mention thousands for captain and crew, servants, soldiers, bow-

60

men, cannoneers, and so forth, which I've paid and continue to pay."

The jungle steamed around us. Don Luis paused to wipe his brow.

"First," he said, "we think of our empty coffers. It won't be long until we are settled on our new island. I heard in Hispaniola that it's a place of surpassing beauty. I'll build there a chapel with many bells and erect a great golden cross for all the Indians to see and wonder at. Be patient, Julián—you'll save many souls."

To this moment in my life I'd had the childish habit of swallowing, like a hungry troutlet, most promises that were offered to me so long as they were seasoned with flattery.

"I've been patient and it has served me ill," I said. "The chapel with many bells and a golden cross would mock me, for I am a seminarian, not a priest, as I have said before. I wish to return to the village of Arroyo and my school. I am heartsick because of what has happened here."

Don Luis squinted. "Ships don't sail every day for the village of Arroyo."

"Then the first that does sail."

"Patience, Julián. You'll still live to be a bishop." He reached in his cloak. "By the way, here's something that I got for you in Hispaniola. It's been blessed by the bishop, by Bishop Zurriaga himself."

He handed me a beautiful rosary of gold beads and a cross encrusted with black pearls.

By noon Señor Guzmán had collected his band, six in all, as well as the lone Indian who knew where his tribe had hidden in the past and where they were apt to hide now, and Esteban, our translator. At the last minute, though he thoroughly mistrusted me, Guzmán decided that I should also go along.

Don Luis and I were standing at the head of the lagoon, watching members of the crew empty the storehouse. He had decided to move the gold onto the *Santa Margarita* in case the camp was overrun by the Caribs. There was danger in this, because the ruffian crew could take it into their heads to sail off with the treasure while we were ashore. But it seemed to be less than the danger from marauding Caribs. There was another and more important reason as well. The *encomendero* who now owned the island might appear and, finding the shed overflowing with gold, rightfully claim it.

Señor Guzmán came up with his band. "We need you," he said, laying a hand on my shoulder. "The savages will believe what you tell them."

"And what will that be?"

"Say that the Caribs have been vanquished, so it's safe to return to their village."

"The Caribs haven't been vanquished," I replied.

Guzmán went on as if I hadn't spoken.

"Say we regret that it was necessary to do away with the cacique."

"It was not necessary."

"I gave him fair warning."

"Why should you warn him? It's his island and his people. Why should you order him to do anything? You are not a king."

Guzmán's mottled face grew pale.

Don Luis said, "We need the men and the women also. We can't mine without them."

Guzmán swallowed hard but went on, "Say that we forgive them for running away. That we'll share the gold they mine; share and share alike."

"You're a friend. They'll listen to you," Don Luis said.

"I have nothing to tell them."

"Say what Guzmán has told you to tell them."

"I would have trouble speaking the words."

"Then say that we need them." He was growing impatient. "Go. Every moment counts."

I did not move.

"You want the Indians back as much as I do."

I spoke slowly so that there would be no doubt about what I was saying. "The truth is, sir, I don't wish them back. I wish them to stay where they are. Wherever it is, they are far better off than here."

Guzmán held in his hand the musket he had used upon the Caribs. He glanced at Don Luis, as if asking his permission to use it at that moment upon me. He had large white teeth, and his drawn-back lips showed that they were clamped tight together.

The young Indian who had given him information about the tribe's whereabouts was watching. He sat huddled on the ground. Around his neck from ear to ear I saw that he bore a thin red welt.

I listened in silence as Don Luis repeated his request.

"You are a member of this expedition," he said. "I, Don Luis de Arroyo, Duke de Cantavara y Llorente, am its leader. I have asked you to accompany us on a mission of great importance. You give me evasive answers."

"What makes you think that our Indians will return to their village if only I speak to them? They have been worked close to death. Some, close to a dozen, have died. Many more have sickened from hard work. And now their chieftain has been cruelly slain. They trust neither you nor Guzmán. They shouldn't trust *me*."

"But they do trust you."

"That, sir, is the point. They trust me, and I will not betray them."

Don Luis smiled, a cold twisting of his lips. "I have always found you a reasonable young man, too serious perhaps, yet upon the whole, of a temperate disposition and not a fool. But this is both intemperate and foolish. You'll bring needless trouble upon yourself."

"As I said and do believe, the tribe is better off in hiding, wherever that may be."

"This is your answer?"

"Yes, sir."

In dismay, Don Luis removed his hat and ran a hand through his hair. "You shall regret this disloyalty," he said. "You shall. You shall."

Señor Guzmán had brought a long coil of rope from the caravel, which I presumed he planned to use to tie up the Indians, should he capture any and they proved unruly. With his sword Don Luis hacked off a length of the rope. Calling to a soldier, he had him bind my hands behind me.

"Escort this young man to the *Santa Margarita*," he said. "Give him over to Captain Roa with instructions to place him in my cabin and see that he remains there."

I was marched thereupon to the beach, loaded into the longboat, and rowed to the caravel, where Don Luis' instructions were carried out to the letter.

I was familiar with Don Luis' cabin, having spent part of every evening there since the beginning of the voyage. Besides a chart table, used for dining, and two chairs bolted tight to the flooring, there was a small sofa, which I had never had the pleasure of using. In the aft bulwark was a large window with thick glass, very old and scratched inside and out. Through it I had a view of the beach, both arms of the bay, and when the caravel turned with the tide, a glimpse of the open sea.

I stood looking out through the hazy glass, watching the longboat return to the lagoon, while I surveyed my problems. At the moment they seemed fairly simple. I couldn't blame Don Luis for my plight, since, as owner of the *Santa Margarita* and leader of the expedition, his fortunes rested upon the blind loyalty of those he commanded. Neither could I blame myself for refusing to obey an order that I felt would betray people who had befriended me.

As for the present, it would be fairly comfortable here in the owner's cabin, bound up though I was. The future? Cloudy. Not hopeless, however. With luck I would find myself on board a caravel bound back to Spain, to Arroyo, and my studies. More than likely Don Luis would be glad to rid himself of my company, of a reminder that he once had had a conscience.

Afternoon clouds piled up and the sky turned black. Then a streak of light broke through and suddenly fell through the window upon the opposite bulwark, placing upon it a crude semblance of a cross. Blinded by what I saw, hastily I got to my knees and said a long prayer of thankfulness and contrition.

But the cross faded away. I was left with an uneasy feeling of unhappiness. The idea that I would be freed and in time find the way home to my village now seemed hollow. The truth was, I'd failed. It was not my fault, perhaps, yet I hadn't done what I had come to the New World to do. I couldn't think of a single person, of one savage soul I had brought to a belief in Christ. Yes, I had failed, and the knowledge of my failure unsettled me.

It came on to thunder. Forked lightning rent the clouds. Rain fell straight down, as it had done every afternoon since we had come to the island.

I wondered how Guzmán and his band were faring. If they brought back the Indians, whether as captives or of their own free will, I would ask for another chance to go among them and speak Christ's message, which in its majesty was meant for all the earth's oppressed, they among them.

The storm blew away. The window was blurred with rain, but I made out our longboat as it left the lagoon and crossed the bay toward us. It sat low in the water, loaded as it was with a heavy cargo. Two men rowed and one sat in the bow.

The latter, I presumed, was Don Luis, but the man turned out to be a middle-aged Sevillano, Alberto Barrios by name. We had been on friendly terms from the first, when he had come to me about a problem he was having with a girl from Cádiz whom he had known for five years yet couldn't make up his mind about marrying. I knew nothing about marriage or girls, especially girls from Cádiz, but I was good at listening, which, as it developed, was all that he really wanted of me.

Barrios was one of the few members of our crew who could be trusted, and so Don Luis had put him in charge of moving the gold. It was stored in baskets with two long handles, which made it possible for several men at once to lift the heavy loads. Gold is very heavy. A piece one and a half spans in all dimensions—a cube, in other words—weighs close upon a ton. The work, therefore, went slowly and took up the rest of the afternoon.

At nightfall I heard steps outside the door, and a figure came in, holding a lantern and a plate of food. The plate was set down in front of me, and by the glow of the lantern I recognized Alberto Barrios.

"I heard you were on board," he said. "Tied up like a chicken."

"Where's Don Luis?"

"With Guzmán. They marched off with the soldiers and both the dogs soon after you were put aboard. Went up the stream, and about an hour after they left I heard the dogs barking and a musket shot. But no news came back, at least while I was at the lagoon."

Barrios had been caught stealing an anchor and sent to prison for ten years, where he served two years before being released by Their Majesties to join our expedition.

"How much gold came aboard?" I asked him, out of curiosity.

"We weighed everything with care, except the small stuff. One nugget came in at sixty libras. And it wasn't larger than your fist. Another, about the size of a small squash, weighed six hundred and twenty libras. Altogether, we weighed more than four thousand. And mind you, it's pure gold. Soft. You can make a dent in it with your thumbnail. There are two more loads as big as the first. We'll handle them tomorrow, providing the sea stays calm. And don't forget that a libra of gold is worth nine hundred pesos."

Barrios went to the window, glanced out at the black night, and came back to stand over me. His eyes glittered in the glow of the ship's lantern.

"You'll have plenty of time," I said. "We'll not see Don Luis for days, perhaps a week."

"But we won't lie around here waiting for him. His instructions were to load everything as fast as possible. He told Captain Roa to raise anchor and stand off the coast when that's done. He's eager to leave the bay before the owner shows up. I saw the gentleman, Olivares is his name, when I was there in Hispaniola, and I'll say that he's not one to sit by and watch someone steal treasure that's his by law."

The caravel strained against her cable, backed off, and began to sway to a gentle creaking of timber.

"The wind," Barrios said.

He glanced at my bound hands but made no move to unbind them.

"It's not a decent way to treat a boy," he said, "a young man who has aspirations, who someday will take holy orders."

He was uneasy. The cabin was too small for him to do much pacing, so instead he kept shifting his weight from one foot to the other. Watching him, I suddenly got the idea that it was not only the wind and weather he was concerned about.

"Don Luis is fast becoming a monster," he said. "He takes after Guzmán, who was born a monster."

It occurred to me that Barrios might be testing my loyalty to Don Luis. If this was true, it could be for only one reason. There must be plans afoot to seize the gold. As soon as it was all on board, the conspirators, under the guise of obeying Don Luis' instructions, would raise anchor and sail the caravel out of the bay. Once out, they would never return.

The cabin began to shift from side to side in a gentle,

wallowing motion. Barrios strode to the window and looked out into the starry night.

"It's the wind again," he said.

I wondered who the conspirators could be. Was it possible that Captain Roa himself was among them? If so, the conspiracy had a good chance of success. Without him? Even then it could succeed.

Barrios had been holding the lantern. He now set it in gimbals above the table. "It's a hot night," he said.

I felt like a martyr of some sort, sitting there with my hands bound. I asked him to untie me.

"I don't have that authority. Not now," he said.

"What do you mean by 'not now'?"

He seemed surprised at my question. "Nothing. Nothing."

We were silent for a while; then Barrios said, "Things happened in Hispaniola when we were there last week. You might want to know, being that you've had dealings with the Indians and like them. It was this way.

"Don Luis came back one afternoon—that was the afternoon of the day we got to Hispaniola—he came back to the caravel after talking to the governor. He was in a bad mood, angry because the governor had turned down his request for Isla del Oro. The man who served his meals he kicked around and he gave the crew a number of daft orders. Then at suppertime, when wine was brought, he got himself in a better mood.

"Roa reminded him that he had dug out a lot of gold, gold worth a hundred thousand pesos, at least. 'Besides,' Roa said, 'you can round up the Indians and take them along to your new *encomienda*. They're worth more than gold.' "

This news astounded me. "It's against the contract of the Indies to handle Indians this way."

"That's what Don Luis said as soon as Roa suggested the idea. Furthermore, breaching of the contract is punishable by death," Barrios explained. "Don Luis knew this. He said that he valued his head since it was the only head he had. But Roa explained how easy it was to evade the law and thereby keep your head."

Barrios went again to the window and came back to report whitecaps on the bay and a rising wind.

A glimmer of suspicion entered my mind. Impatiently, I waited for him to continue.

"You evade the law by causing the Indians to revolt," he continued. "You do this by working them too hard, or not paying them the few centavos required by law, or just lopping off a few heads. If Indians do revolt and flee into the jungle, according to the law, you can go after them and bring them back. Henceforth and for the rest of their lives, they are slaves and belong to you, to use or to sell as you wish. It's a common practice. The Indies could not prosper without it. But if it continues, all the Indians will be dead or enslaved."

I got to my feet. We looked at each other across the table. His eyes shining in the glare of the swaying lantern, Barrios studied my face.

"Where is Don Luis now?" he said in an angry tone, and chose to answer his own question. "Chasing Indians, that's where he is. Why is he chasing Indians? Be-

71

cause the Indians revolted and fled into the jungle and he needs them to work the mine, the mine that isn't his. And why did the Indians flee? Because Guzmán worked them until they were sick and then set the big dog on their leader and mangled him to death."

I kept the horror to myself. "I believe you," I said, scarcely able to form the words.

"I speak the truth."

"Then what I saw at that moment when the dog was loosed was not just murder caused by anger. It was worse, far worse. It was murder planned and thought about. It was murder born of greed, done coldly and deliberately."

Barrios nodded.

He went to the window for a third time and peered out, shading his eyes against the glare of the lantern. "Surf's running high. We won't be able to use the *lancha* tomorrow. But I'll load the gold if I have to swim and carry it piece by piece."

Barrios didn't ask me to join the conspiracy that was plainly afoot, but as he left the cabin he unbound my hands, saying that before long I might need them.

At dawn, amid a violent storm of wind and rain, Barrios seized the *Santa Margarita*. Captain Roa was bound hand and foot and put away in a cubbyhole below deck next to the stable. Unbound, I was allowed the freedom of Don Luis' cabin, but a sentry armed with a saber stood outside my door.

The storm lasted two days and two nights. On the morning of the third day, under blue skies, the crew set off for the lagoon. Barrios had decided to transport the remaining two loads of gold to the beach by muleback and there put it on the *lancha* for the short trips to the caravel, thus saving valuable time. And time was valuable to Barrios, for Don Luis and Guzmán could be expected at any hour, as could the owner of the island, the gentleman from Hispaniola, Señor Olivares.

During the two days of the storm I hadn't lacked for comforts. I ate what the crew ate, but from time to time Barrios brought me extra viands that he had set aside for himself, including a slice of goat cheese, slightly overripe, five sea biscuits, which officially we'd run out of weeks before, and a small pot of excellent orange conserve he had brought along from Seville, made, he said, by the girl from Cádiz.

I felt somewhat like a pig being fattened for slaughter, though I knew that the small gifts were meant to curry favor. Even if I chose, there was little I could do to interfere with the mutiny, but Barrios liked me and wanted to feel that what he was doing I understood and sympathized with.

Besides, more than likely he was looking ahead to a dire possibility that someday he might be haled before a court and asked to explain how he had come into possession of a caravel loaded with gold. A young witness of good reputation, willing to testify in his behalf, could save his treasure as well as his neck.

And should that happen, if before a court in Hispaniola or in Spain I was called upon for testimony in his behalf, I would give it. Neither the gold nor the caravel belonged to him. He had stolen both. He was a thief.

And yet my horror at what Don Luis had done was so overpowering that I could almost see myself standing before a court, swearing to tell the truth and then not telling it.

For an hour after dawn there was no movement aboard the *Santa Margarita*. Occasionally I heard my guard, a sailor named Luna, mumble a word or two. Now and then he walked away, I presumed to take a closer look at the bay and the sea.

The caravel herself swung at anchor, quietly turning her stern toward the shore as the tide ran in.

I had a good view of the bay. For the first hour after Barrios and the crew went off, there was movement neither on the beach nor along the fringe of the jungle.

Then, as the tide ebbed, and there was no sound except the crying of the gulls, I heard a single cannon shot. It was followed shortly by a volley of musket fire. Then it was quiet again.

I called through the door and asked Luna if he saw anything.

"Nothing," he replied. *"Nada."*

"There's a fight somewhere," I said.

"The noise comes from the lagoon."

"The muskets and cannon both?"

"Both."

"I have only a view of the bay," I said. "What do you find otherwise?"

"Otherwise nothing. I can see far out. It is very clear on the ocean."

"No sails? A caravel is expected."

"No sails. No caravel. *Nada.*"

As I peered through the window, I pictured in my mind a scene at the lagoon. Barrios and the crew were in the act of loading the last of the gold on the mules, making ready to start off for the beach, when Don Luis and Guzmán with their men came out of the jungle. I decided that they had failed to find the Indians and were in an angry mood. Barrios would explain that he and the crew had already moved a boatload of gold to the *Santa Margarita* and would have moved all of it except for the storm. No further explanation would be needed until Don Luis arrived on the caravel and found Captain Roa bound hand and foot.

At that moment, Barrios, who was not dull-witted,

would say that the captain had tried to seize the caravel and sail off with her, but that he, Barrios, had stood staunchly against it. Captain Roa would deny this, but Barrios would be backed up promptly by the crew and by me.

As events turned out, as the true story unfolded piece by piece, I was proved wrong. Don Luis and his men did march out of the jungle while the crew was busy loading gold. But they came with thirty Indians— twenty-seven men and three women, one of them carrying a child—captured after a bloody fight in a canyon at the head of the stream. They had captured more, but five of the Indians died of wounds on the march back to the lagoon.

Barrios and the crew were surprised, but instead of acting as I thought they would, several members of the crew took fright and bolted into the jungle, choosing to take their chances with the Indians rather than with Guzmán. The rest meekly submitted, all except Barrios, who told the story I imagined he might tell. It was received with a howl of laughter by Don Luis and by Guzmán, who felled him with one thrust of his sword.

The first I knew of this was about an hour later, while I stood peering out of the cabin window. The caravel had shifted with the tide, which was now running seaward, so I had only a partial view of the island.

Six mules plodded along the beach, followed by soldiers and members of the crew. Next came a long, straggling line of naked Indians, then a band of musketmen. Mounted on horses, Don Luis and Guzmán brought up the rear.

The line looked like a big ungainly snake, winding its way down the narrow strip of sand between the jungle and the sea. The Indians slowly walked along, one after the other, bound together, the man in front bound to the man behind by a single length of ship's rope that encircled the neck of each. One man couldn't flee unless all fled. If one man stumbled or stopped, it caused trouble everywhere along the line.

Just such trouble took place as the Indians approached the longboat.

My view wasn't good, but I saw the line suddenly buckle, buckle and stop, then move forward, then stop again. Somewhere in the middle of the line an Indian, a man with gray hair, had been overcome by exhaustion, or perhaps by fear, as he saw the caravel riding at anchor and fully realized his fate. In any event, he fell to his knees, struggled to get up, but failed.

Guzmán, who had ridden forward as soon as the line came to a halt, sat above the fallen man, looking down at him in contempt. He must have shouted some command, for the Indian grasped at the air and strained to get to his feet, but again fell to his knees. With one hand on the peak of his saddle, Guzmán reached down and swung his saber. The rope severed, the old man's head flew off and rolled into the surf. Thus freed of the encumbering body, the Indians moved on.

I noticed two gaps along the length of rope where men had stood with their necks encircled, so I concluded that Guzmán had dealt with them in the same manner.

As the line reached the boat waiting on the beach,

cries went up that clearly reached me above the noise of the surf. The Indians looked wildly about, and for a moment I thought that surely they would try to break their bonds and flee. But the soldiers stood with weapons ready, while Don Luis rode around the huddled group, making gestures that were meant to calm them.

I watched in disbelief.

I had heard Las Casas speak of horrors dealt to the gentle people of the Indies, but his words, forceful as they were, had not prepared me for what was taking place at this very moment, for what had taken place in the past—men and women forced to labor until they sickened, the cacique Ayo mangled to death by a vicious dog, men and women pursued, captured, and led into captivity by a rope around their necks, beheaded if they faltered.

How could other men who prayed upon their knees, beseeching God's mercy, begging for His protection, swearing that in gratitude they would honor Him by spreading His word among the islands of the Indies— how could these Christian men commit such acts of brutality?

Mercifully, my view of the beach and the huddled Indians, who now were waiting until the gold could be carried aboard, was suddenly closed off as the caravel shifted with the tide.

Confronted for the first time in my life by the bare face of evil, I closed my eyes and prayed for guidance. Before I could compose my spirit, however, Luna, the guard, opened the door and stared at me, his face white with fear.

He said, "They have come back. Don Luis and Guzmán. Everyone except Señor Barrios. Since the mutiny was not of my making, they have no reason to blame me."

"They don't need a reason," I said. "Hide your musket and we'll go and untie Captain Roa. That should put a better face on the situation."

deck, kept a watchful eye upon their movements as well as upon the horizon to the east.

The gold—gold in pieces the size of oranges, gold in flakes and slivers, in nuggets the shape of nutmegs—all this was placed in neat rows for everyone to see. The hot sun shone upon it, blinding the eyes.

When all the treasure was unloaded and lay upon the deck, Don Luis gave orders for the savages to be brought aboard. They came quietly, five boatloads of them, guarded by soldiers. They were put in the hold among the water casks and empty stalls. When the animals were brought aboard, it would be crowded.

Don Luis then called his henchmen and all members of the crew to the main deck. He had not taken time to change his torn attire or clean the blood from his face. He stood amidst the treasure, with Señor Guzmán at his side, and said pridefully to all those assembled:

"I have kept the solemn promise I gave you many months ago in the city of Seville, as we set off with God's guidance to face the dangers of the New World. I promised you gold, and here it lies in front of you. In a moment of weakness, some of you listened to bad counsel and were led astray. This, though it broke the laws of land and sea and should have cost you your lives, I have forgiven."

I wondered, as I stood listening apart from the crowd, if his decision to spare the crew's lives was prompted less by mercy than the most certain knowledge that without a crew the caravel couldn't sail more than ten leagues even in fair weather.

"Your share, however, will be less," he went on, "yet

a goodly portion. Each crewman will receive twenty libras of gold—to be weighed out here on deck by Señor Guzmán—at this moment. Any differences in weight must be adjusted among yourselves. In other words, do not come back complaining of false weight. Complaining, indeed, of anything."

Each of the crew stepped forward and received his share. There was no grumbling, at least none that I heard, for each of them must have remembered that he'd had a close encounter with death. Don Luis' retainers were then called forward to claim their share of the treasure, which was twice the amount accorded to the crew.

Throughout this ceremony, a low-pitched chant rose from the hold. I understood none of the words, except that the name of Ayo, the dead cacique, was repeated over and over.

I looked around for Esteban and, seeing that he was busy with a game of dice, went alone to the hold. The Indians were huddled together in a stall that had stabled two of our mules, animals that had died during the first week we were on the island. With room to sit but not to move about, they squatted shoulder to shoulder, rocking as they chanted.

The chant stopped when I appeared. I saw the gleam of eyes in the dim light. One of the women had a child, and the child began to cry. There was no other sound except the tramping of feet overhead.

The silence grew. Ayo's people, my friends, waited for me to speak, but there was nothing I could say, not in words they would understand. Nor that I could say in their own words, if I had known the words. In truth, it was not a time for words.

Powerless, with a feeling of humiliation, I knelt in the stable straw and tried to pray. My lips moved, sounds came from my throat, but my thoughts never left my body, never left the hole where we all huddled in the half-darkness.

While I was there on my knees, Moreno, the black-smith, came down from above to say that Don Luis wanted me on deck. He carried a lantern in one hand and held his nose with the other, for the stink of the stable, which the crew had been too busy to clean after the long voyage, was sickening. I took the lantern from him and held it out to Pital, a young man with whom I had sometimes traded words.

Pital took the lantern and held it above his head. The wick flickered with a small, dull flame, but it was fire that, if so minded, he could use to set the stable straw ablaze and burn to the water's edge the unholy *Santa Margarita.*

When I went on deck, the sun was setting and a soft breeze blew in from the island. The crew and the retain-ers were scattered around fore and aft, and, except for the two lookouts high in the tower, were gambling with dice, wagering the gold they had just acquired.

Don Luis stood on the main deck beside his pile of treasure, which still reached above his head. His hands were on his hips, his booted feet thrust apart, and he smiled as he beckoned me forward.

"I'm pleased to see that you have untied yourself," he said in a friendly voice, as if not he but someone else had given the order that tied me up. "I acted hastily. Come and claim your share of the treasure."

"I haven't earned a share," I said.

"As much as anyone. *Venga.* Come."

He must have thought that I was acting out of modesty, for he repeated his command. When I didn't move, he reached down, scooped up a double handful of nuggets, strode forward, and with a bow pressed them into my hands.

The nuggets were heavy. They weighed twenty libras or more—enough gold to keep me in books for many years to come. I put them in my purse.

The longboat was on shore, loading the mastiffs, horses, and mules. Before night fell, the animals would be in their stalls, and the Indians would be without so much as a place to lie. I thought about Barrios and the girl in Cádiz who would never see him again. I thought of Ayo, the cacique, lying dead somewhere in the jungle. The Indians were chanting again. I remembered the lantern I had given Pital and wondered if he would have the courage to use it.

A lookout called down from his lofty perch in the mainmast crow's-nest and reported a sail.

"East by northeast," he shouted, "bearing down under full canvas."

The caravel came suddenly alive under Señor Guzmán's loud curses. The first of the animals moved aboard in a hurry and were shoved and coaxed into the hold, and the longboat went back for more. The full crew took their stations, ready, as soon as the last of the beasts were on board, to weigh anchor. The lookout, in answer to Captain Roa, estimated that the caravel would not reach us for another hour.

I went to the hold and found that the Indians were crouching among the horses, the lantern in their midst. Apparently, they were not going to use it to free themselves.

I climbed the ladder and walked in the darkness to the rail. Without being seen, I unfastened from my belt the purse filled with gold nuggets and dropped it into the dark waters of the bay.

An hour later, with everything stowed and a full moon rising, the *Santa Margarita* weighed anchor and moved out of the bay on a fair land breeze.

The caravel the lookout had sighted earlier now loomed bright in the moon glow, close off our port bow. Señor Guzmán wished to send a cannonball into her rigging, but Captain Roa persuaded him otherwise and we headed southeasterly on a new course, toward the land His Majesty had graciously granted to *encomendero* Don Luis de Arroyo, Duke of Cantavara y Llorente, which he had already named Isla de Buenaventura.

The next morning the sun rose in a reddish haze. The sea was the same red color as the sky. Captain Roa said that the weather signs tempted him to wish he was not on an overburdened vessel, but somewhere far away, like the city of Seville.

He was speaking to Don Luis as they stood on the afterdeck, drinking their morning chocolate. Don Luis, except for a few scratches, looked no worse for his exploits in the jungle. His beard was curled and his hip-boots polished. He wore a soft, sleeveless doublet, yellow in color, cured with ambergris, in the latest mode.

"We carry far too much weight," said Captain Roa. "Three tons of gold and twenty-nine slaves give us at least five tons more than when we sailed from Seville. It puts a heavy strain upon mast and timber."

Off our starboard bow, as the captain spoke, there appeared a small verdant isle indented by a bay well protected from the wind. He pointed to the shelter and suggested to Don Luis that we might drop anchor and ride out the wind, should one develop.

Don Luis said, "What are the chances of a wind?"

"Unfortunately, great," said the captain. "I have observed the portents before. Thin clouds moving westward. A red dawn. A sea without so much as a ripple."

"If the wind arrives, how long does it last?"

"Five days. Six. I recall one that lasted for a week and more. That was during the last voyage of Columbus. In fifteen-o-two, the Governor of Hispaniola, Don Nicolás de Ovando, arrived in San Domingo with an armada of thirty sail, all loaded with treasure and ready to depart for Spain. I was on one of his ships, the *Aguja.* My first voyage as boatswain."

The captain stopped suddenly and pointed toward the stretch of water between us and the small island.

"You'll notice," he said, taking Don Luis' arm, "the number of dolphins swimming on the surface. Another sign of a coming storm."

"You were discussing Don Nicolás de Ovando," Don Luis said, looking at the captain, not at the sea. "And his armada. Someday I will have one as large."

"Ovando's ships," the captain continued, "were anchored at the mouth of the Ozama River. Columbus stood at the entrance to the harbor and asked permission to enter. Out of jealousy and arrogance, Ovando refused him. At the same time portents of a storm appeared, like those that I have just observed this morning. Despite the shabby treatment he had received from Ovando, Columbus warned him not to send the armada to sea. Ovando sneered at the Admiral, scoffed at his advice, and the rich armada sailed. They were out less than a day when the hurricane struck. All of the thirty ships were sunk or wrecked on shore, except my ship, the *Aguja.* More than five hundred men were drowned."

"What happened to Columbus?" I asked.

"He moved his ships not to the harbor but close in

upon the land," said the captain, "and rode out the wind."

Captain Roa must have chosen this story deliberately, but he had chosen it wrongly. The story of the catastrophe at San Domingo with its horrendous loss of treasure and life served only as a challenge to Don Luis. Unlike Nicolás de Ovando, Governor of Hispaniola and Knight Commander of Lares, he was protected by his own unbending will, his strong right arm, and by God's most certain grace.

"If we seek shelter whenever a wind blows," Don Luis said, "the year ends before we make Buenaventura. By the way, Captain, how far does it lie?"

"Three days off if the weather stays fair."

"More, if we chance to miss our landfall. We have missed it once already."

"A fortunate miss," Captain Roa reminded him, putting a sharp edge on his words. He was in a bad mood, not having recovered from the severe buffeting received at the hands of the crew. "Worth the cost of the caravel and more."

"True, true," said Don Luis. "My thanks, my thanks."

"And speaking of the gold," the captain continued, "but not of the slaves, who are worth five hundred excelentes. Speaking of the gold, I am the only one on the *Santa Margarita* who has not received his share."

"Not by an oversight," Don Luis assured him. "Once we reach our island I'll see to it. That was our agreement, if you remember."

"But we may never reach the island. I have many

doubts about how the *Santa Margarita* will act in a wind. The old tub may shake apart. Turn her belly to the sky."

"If she does, what good will the gold do you?"

"At least I'll have had the pleasure of being rich, if only for a moment."

Don Luis smiled. "This being your wish, I hereby present you with all the gold you can carry away."

"I have a very weak back," said the captain.

"Then make two trips," Don Luis replied. "Three. But in the meantime, let us move along and not tarry at every passing shelter that invites us."

The sails had been slack all morning. Now a strong gust of wind filled them, and the *Santa Margarita* began to make headway.

"Furthermore," said Don Luis, "adventurers swarm about the court in Spain, begging Their Majesties for grants to isles, to reefs and rivers, even to continents. They swarm through the governor's palace in Hispaniola—I saw them there by the dozens—asking for *encomiendas*. They sail the seas like hungry sharks looking for pieces of land to bite off. The sooner we make our island and settle ourselves upon it, the more comfortable rests my mind."

Captain Roa chewed the ends of his mustache and looked down at the deck. As he had before, at the time we ran low on water and he advised Don Luis that it was wise to return to the Canaries, he once more went against his better judgment. We had been saved then by great good fortune. I wondered if we would be saved again.

"We sail," said the captain. "But the gold needs to be shifted. Here on deck it makes us top-heavy. In a wind we'll rock like a baby's cradle."

Don Luis said, "I don't trust the crew to handle the treasure, even from here to the hold."

"Nor I," said the captain.

Guzmán had appeared and stood listening. He wore a bandage over one of his ears, a part of which had been severed but which Juan Pacheco, barber and surgeon, had restored.

"How the crew long to get their claws into it," he said. "Sorry lot that they are. We'd be better off if they were ten fathoms under."

"Where do we store the gold?" Don Luis asked.

"In the stable," said the captain.

"Not with the horses."

"With the savages."

"Yes, let them sit on it. They can serve as watchmen."

Now that the sun had risen and everyone was on deck, except the Indians, without much spirit I sang a morning song. Afterward, Don Luis asked me to go below and repeat the song for the savages.

"Let them know," he said, "that they have nothing to fear. In three days they shall be living on a beautiful island. Give the mother comfort and her child this sweetmeat." He drew forth from his doublet a hard, yellow confection and put it in my hand. "And you should take with you the picture of the Virgin Mother and Child. I noticed in the past when we first came to the island that the savages displayed great interest in the holy picture when you showed it to them."

"I fear that now they'll show little interest," I said. "If I were they, I wouldn't feel any. Therefore, I shall not take the picture. Nor will I make them promises about life on a beautiful island. But I will give the sweetmeat to the child, if you wish, and say it is from God. If I said it was a gift from you, the mother wouldn't allow her child to take it. For which I would not blame her."

Don Luis brushed a mosquito from his sleeve. "You are very stiff-necked about these slaves. I recall that you are an admirer of Las Casas. I've heard you speak of him. I believe he preached in our village church on one occasion. You took leave of school to attend."

He waited for me to say something, and when I didn't, he went on.

"But I have never heard you mention the fact that this Las Casas, who is highly regarded by both Their Majesties and by the Church, proposed that Negroes be shipped from Africa to the Indies. It was his idea and it is now being carried out. They are captured in Africa by slave-hunters, transported to Hispaniola, and sold here to the highest bidders for work on the farms."

"I am aware of this," I said. "Las Casas was wrong. What you are doing is wrong also. Enslaving the Indians. Taking gold that does not belong to you."

Don Luis showed his teeth in a quick smile. "You were glad enough to take a share of the gold," he taunted me.

"Not glad," I said. "The gold you pressed upon me I threw away. It's now at the bottom of the sea."

Don Luis was carrying his sword. It hadn't left his side since he came aboard yesterday. I am sure that last night he had slept with the sword. His hand settled upon the hilt. Our eyes met. I am certain from what I saw there that it took the whole of his will power not to slip the sword from its sheath and run me through.

"With your permission," I said, being as respectful to him as to any of my elders, as I had been taught to be by a strict father, "I will go."

I left him mumbling something or other about ingratitude and went to gather up Esteban. I located him playing tarok, holding in one hand the last of his nuggets, and dragged him off to the companionway.

The verdant isle and its sheltering bay dropped astern. As we reached the hold, a slow, surging wave lifted the caravel and tilted her to starboard. She hung there, then timbers groaned as the old vessel righted herself, swung slowly to port, then little by little moved back to an even keel.

The hold smelled of sadness. The Indians were huddled together, holding each other, sick. I felt sick myself.

When Esteban and I left the huddled Indians, in our short time away from the deck, the sky had changed color. The thin, white clouds that seemed driven by a high wind were now gray. While we stood at the head of the ladder, the gray deepened to black, the black became a greenish blue. Night was close upon us.

Long, surging swells were moving in from southeastward, but the surface of the sea was unruffled and oily, like a vast dark stone. The air was still.

A lookout in the mainmast tower called down that he had raised two large islands. From the sterncastle, Captain Roa called back and asked where they lay.

"Off our starboard bow. Three degrees."

"At what distance?"

"Four leagues, give or take."

Whereupon Captain Roa instructed the helmsman to head the *Santa Margarita* south by southeastward. At the command, Don Luis hurried out of his quarters, wanting to know why our course had been changed.

Captain Roa said, "We are within an hour's sailing of likely islands. In that time we may well be in need of their shelter. The storm lies close at hand. Its portents increase by the moment."

Don Luis glanced at the overcast sky, the calm, unruffled sea, the dolphin swimming just below the surface of the water—all the signs the captain had spoken of before—but again he stubbornly refused to heed them.

Señor Guzmán came from below, where he had talked to the crew. Speaking in his gentlest voice, which was only a tone less than a shout, he said to Don Luis, "The men are for putting in at the next island."

"And what," Don Luis asked, "has the crew to do with how we sail and where we sail?"

"Everything," said Guzmán. "We are on a ship with a storm fast approaching."

"Two days ago, the moment you learned that they had mutinied, you were of a mind to kill them all."

"A mistake, sir." Señor Guzmán never addressed Don Luis as "sir" except when he was angry. "A mistake which I regret."

"It's also a mistake to allow them to run the ship," said Don Luis.

The crew, those on watch and those who had been asleep or gambling, had gathered on the main deck, just below the sterncastle, where we stood. The men carried no weapons except their tough fists. At least none that I observed.

Don Luis glanced down at them and made a quick count, mumbling the numbers as he counted. There were nine men, with two missing. A dangerous lot, he must have thought, their appetite for gold only whetted by what he had given them, anxious for anything to happen. Even a shipwreck, so long as they would benefit.

His own small army of soldiers, cannoneers, bowmen,

and musketeers were not in sight, but they weren't in hiding. They were loyal, he knew, and would support him with their weapons and their lives.

A gust of steaming air swept the deck; then came a short lull and in a moment or two a second gust, this one stronger and from a different direction.

Don Luis was silent, his hand on the hilt of his sword. He glanced at Señor Guzmán and Captain Roa, at the crew standing sullenly by the main-deck hatch. He started to speak and stopped, then asked the cabin boy to fetch Juan Pacheco.

Pacheco came running with comb and curling iron, thinking that his master's beard was in need of attention. But Don Luis sent him back for his astrological materials.

"Tell me," Don Luis said, when Pacheco, barber, surgeon, reader of the heavens, returned with parchment, inkhorn, and quill, "what signs govern our fortune on this day in August in the land and on the seas of New Spain?"

"Be patient, Señor Don Luis," said the barber, as if he were speaking to a child, in a tone his master would not countenance from anyone else, "and I will cast you a full and all-embracing chart."

"It need not be all-embracing," Don Luis replied. "We lack time to embrace everything."

The barber glanced in the direction of the sun, which was hidden behind a bank of clouds. He asked Captain Roa if he knew the day of the *Santa Margarita*'s launching.

"The twenty-first of May," said the captain. "In fourteen ninety-one. There's a plaque on board that gives that date and year."

"At what hour?"

Captain Roa thought for a while and said that she had slipped down the ways exactly at noon, a detail he must have made up on the moment.

Pacheco mumbled something to himself, saying, "A happy placement of the planet Mercury."

My grandfather, God elevate and preserve his soul, was devoted to the art of astrology, even though he was a devout man. In fact, the movements of planets, of the sun, moon, and the stars as they swung through the heavens controlled his earthly life from hour to hour and day to day.

If in the morning, having studied his charts, he found there to be danger connected with fire, he would not light the kitchen stove nor go near it. If the stars said that the day was poor for planting, he would remain in the house, far from the fields. Keen was his disappointment that I showed only a small interest in the subject.

Pacheco looked at the sky. A bluish green light sifted down from above, spreading over the sea and the ship and the faces of all the men. He paced back and forth, staring at the surging waves and lowering sky, at the slow rise and fall of the *Santa Margarita*'s prow.

"Come," he said. "The crew shows too much curiosity." The barber, with his quill and inkhorn, started toward the cabin. When I didn't follow, Don Luis said to me, "You also, Julián." He motioned Captain Roa and Guzmán away.

I went with the greatest of reluctance. The idea that these two men held in their hands the fate of the ship and of all our lives appalled me. That our fate could rest upon the movement of heavenly bodies and the barber's readings thereof was against all the teachings of the holy fathers in my seminary.

The cabin was in shadow. Little light came through the window, but that little had the same strange cast as the light that fell upon the sea and the ship.

From somewhere, Don Luis brought forth a small book bound in red leather and handed it over to Pacheco. In Arroyo the barber had a book of his own filled with astrological lore, a tome as big as a loaf of bread, which, when it was not in use, he wisely kept out of sight under a pile of moldy straw in the strawloft.

He now seated himself at the table, removed the stopper from the inkhorn, spread out a soiled square of parchment, and put down several notations, apparently the details that Captain Roa had just given him.

I had the impression as I stood watching Pacheco that he had done this many times during the voyage. It was probable that some or all of Don Luis' pig-headed decisions had been based upon information Pacheco had drawn down from the starry skies.

As the barber continued with his writing, Don Luis grew impatient. He brushed me aside, went to the window, and glanced out, saying over his shoulder, "What do you find, not about me but about the *Santa Margarita*?"

We found Captain Roa in the deepest part of the caravel, lying upon a pile of dirty straw, seemingly more
dead than alive. But when we unloosed his bindings and
gave him the news that the mutiny was over, he quickly
revived.

As well he might, for he was aware that his life had
been spared by Barrios solely because he was a passable
navigator. Once the caravel and its treasure neared its
destination, Barrios would have put an end to him.
Events had saved Captain Roa, but he thanked us with
a great show of gratitude, as if we alone were responsible for his good fortune.

The three of us mounted to the main deck, arriving
there just as the longboat, stacked with gold from gunwale to gunwale, ranged alongside. In the bow stood
Don Luis, his fine chain and leather doublet torn, and
his face a mass of scratches. He smiled up at me, as if
nothing had happened between us, and raised his sword
triumphantly. He looked like a true conquistador, a
conqueror, a man of honor. For a moment I forgot what
he had done, and all that he had permitted to be done
in his name.

Five members of the crew who had arrived in the
longboat set about carrying the gold aboard, prodded
along by Don Luis, who, from a perch above the main

"At this time," said the barber, "you are the *Santa Margarita.* I am also. We all are. At this hour, ship and man share the same fate."

"*Hombre,* this I know," said Don Luis. "Don't be fancy with your readings. We lack time for fanciness; for quibbling, likewise."

I went to the door and looked out. The ship had been moving on a light wind that came upon us in gusts. Now the wind had faded and the sails hung limp. I heard beneath me the groan of the heavy rudder, the creak of planks and oaken ribs.

Pacheco continued with his writing.

Don Luis left the window and, again brushing me aside, glanced out the door. "*Venga!*" he shouted. "Tell me what you see and do not put a pretty face on things."

"I see," said Juan Pacheco, barber, surgeon, astrologer, and soothsayer, "a long voyage for the *Santa Margarita* into uncharted waters, past many island empires, where gold abundantly exists, a voyage under fair skies and foul."

"God's body!" exploded Don Luis. "Tell me what I have not already seen."

Pacheco apparently did not hear him. He closed the book, glanced at his writings, and with bowed head spoke softly to himself in muffled words that sounded like an incantation. Don Luis stood over him, listening, his face colored by the strange light cast down from the skies.

I had never seen the devil before, in all my sixteen years, but for a moment I saw him then. He was standing there in place of Don Luis, bending over one of his infernal servants, listening to words that should not be spoken in the light of day.

"What do you want?" I cried. "Why am I here?"

Don Luis straightened up and looked at me as if he had forgotten that I was there in the cabin. He thought for a while. "You are here to intercede with God, to whom we shall commend our souls."

The vision did not fade. The devil himself stood there. Pacheco's incantations went on. Then Don Luis told him to cease and turned to me with clasped hands and a pious gaze.

I backed away from him. "Pray for yourself!" I cried out. As I opened the door and slammed it shut, muffled sounds mocked me.

On deck Captain Roa gave orders to place all the animals in heavy rope slings lest the coming storm pound them to death. He called aloft and asked the lookout how far the islands' shelter lay. They were near, but in the black night that now descended upon us we somehow passed them.

Stealthily, like a highwayman in the dark, the hurricane fell upon us.

In midmorning, as I stood beside the after hatch, with a crash that seemed to come from all directions at once, I was enveloped in a torrent of air. Sails, large and small, blew out with the roar of cannon shot. They instantly became streaming ribbons that pointed in the direction we now were driven, which was headlong into the west.

On hands and knees I clawed my way across the deck, certain that the next moment I would be swept away.

I reached the railing at the head of the companionway, hung there until I got my breath and my bearings, then, with a lurch of the ship, fell sprawling into the hold. I landed in the midst of the crew and Don Luis' servants, who were huddled at the foot of the ladder. In the dim light, silent with fear, they looked like statues.

Captain Roa, who had called them down from mast and deck moments before the hurricane struck, helped me to my feet.

"The ship is helpless," he said calmly. "And we are helpless. Only God, if He mercifully chooses, can save us all."

His words brought us to life.

Pedro Esquivel, the caulker, tore open his shirt and,

placing his hand upon his bare chest, swore that if God did save him he would crawl like a worm to the nearest shrine. Bustamente, a soldier, cried out that he would go naked as the day he was born through the crowded streets of Seville to the great cathedral.

I prayed for all our company. At Captain Roa's bidding I quoted the passage in the Bible about the tempest of Capernaum, which ends with "It is I; be not afraid." I prayed especially for the Indians hidden away in the stalls.

Captain Roa put three men on the pump, since water now sloshed around us, ankle-deep. The animals, held in slings, were pawing their stalls, so he sent men to give them fodder that had been taken from the island. Those at the rudder he relieved and had the oaken tiller lashed down, for it could not be handled. To Señor Guzmán and five of the crew he gave the task of transporting the gold from the deck to the hold, which was done by dropping it down the companionway.

Two of the men were drowned at the task, and the shifting of the gold made no difference in the motion of the ship. She staggered and rolled just the same from beam end to beam end.

Without sails, under bare poles, she drove westward through the afternoon while the wind roared and rain fell and thunderous waves pounded her hull. She seemed, I swear, to move in circles, yet at nightfall we faced a setting sun that eerily and unexpectedly appeared from under the scudding clouds. To a band of silent men I sang the Salve Regina.

Soon after sunset the rudder jumped its gudgeons.

101

But as if nothing had happened, the ship drove onward into the west.

It was an hour or so later, during a lull in the wind, that I heard an unusual sound. At first I thought it came from the hold, where the animals were stabled. But after a moment when the sound was repeated I felt certain that it came from the forecastle and that it was the cry of a child in distress.

Toward midnight the wind no longer roared. It now came upon us in shrieks, pausing, then often on a higher note, shrieking again. Sebastián Lomas of the midnight watch reported that the Indians had left the hold and gone. He had seen them climb the forecastle companionway and, one by one, silently hurl themselves into the sea.

Just before dawn, Guzmán ventured above and returned with the news that the masts still stood, the wind had lessened and changed direction, and land lay both on our port and starboard. Captain Roa sent men to repair the rudder and chose a watch to set two small sails as soon as dawn broke.

While the crew huddled at the companionway, waiting to go on deck, I led them in prayer. Afterward, I prayed for the Indians, closing my heart and thoughts to the pain they must have endured, to the cries of the child in distress, to the despair that drove them into the sea.

It was soon after that the caravel rose by the bow, as if lifted by a monstrous hand. At the same moment a tumultuous blow knocked us all from our feet, and through a gaping hole amidships, raging water rushed in upon us.

Those who were not drowned by the rushing water escaped to the main deck. There were six of us. The sky was dark, but eastward the first light shone.

I found myself in the sea, gasping for breath, in a trough between two waves. One wave left me and the other lifted me high. There could have been other men around me, but I saw only two—the pinched face of Juan Pacheco and the bushy red hair of Don Luis.

Luis was clinging to a length of timber, which looked to be a piece of the mainmast. It was not big enough to support both men, and as the barber reached out to grasp it, Don Luis pushed his hand away.

From the crest of the wave that bore me upward, I saw in one direction the outline of what seemed to be a rocky, continuous coast. Somewhat to the south was an island fringed by jungle and a palely gleaming beach. The coast was almost a league away; the island not that far, perhaps half the distance.

Out of instinct I set off for the island, lost now in drifting spray. Having been raised by the banks of the Guadalquivir, I was a good swimmer, but a river is not a gale-whipped sea, and I was forced to the limits of my strength.

I had gone no farther than halfway toward the beach when I heard a scream behind me. It came from one of our horses, the black stallion Bravo. He was pawing the air, head reared high and his long mane streaming in the wind.

For a moment, as a wave lifted us heavenward, I thought that he was about to swim back toward the place the ship had gone down, now marked by the top part of her mainmast. I shouted his name, shouted it twice, shouted it a third time. Whether he heard my voice or not, the stallion turned his head away from the wreck.

He swam after me as I struggled toward the island, over towering waves that sped me along, through shallows, and at last tumbled me upon the shining beach.

Bruised and belabored, I lay there I know not how long, awakening at last with a brilliant sun in my eyes.

I got to my feet and searched myself for injuries. Finding none, I climbed to a jutting rock, the shoulder of the reef upon which the *Santa Margarita* had foundered, and whose height offered a chance to survey my surroundings.

I reached this flat eminence with difficulty and once there sat for a long time before having the desire to look about me. A blinding glare rose from the sea, so I was unable to make out the wreck or the coast or anything that stood to the east. I turned my back to the rising sun and, feature by feature, took in all that lay immediately around, to the south and north and the west.

The beach was crescent-shaped, the far point of the crescent ending in a high, jutting rock similar to the one I stood upon, flat on top and whitened by a myriad of sea fowl, many of whom now sailed above my head. Not protesting my presence, they seemed, on the contrary, bent upon welcoming me to their island home with soft cries.

Southward of the rock I stood upon stretched a blue-green jungle, as solid-seeming as if carved from stone. In the distance, two or three leagues northward, I made out the shape of a lone mountain. It was heavily wooded for two thirds of its height, and from this point upward was rust-colored and treeless. From its summit issued a plume of gray smoke that trailed away on the wind. I had never seen one before, but judging from what I had read, this mountain that towered into the sky was a live volcano.

Beyond it the jungle stretched, as far as I could see, for several leagues in one unbroken wave of trees and brush. To the west, except for an expanse of meadow, there lay country in no way different from that to the north and south.

The shelving beach below me led to a broad band of marsh grass. This band bordered on the seaward side a meadow that must have been half a league in circumference, round in shape as if someone had so arranged it, and cut by a stream that meandered out of the jungle and, in a series of shallow loops, reached the shore. Here it fanned out into a broad estuary and the sea.

The edges of the meadow where it met the jungle were spotted with spiky plants that sent up shafts of scarlet flowers. The rest was lush grass, light green in color, which came to the stallion's belly as he stood grazing.

With the wide sea at my back and faced on three sides by unbroken jungle, I felt completely lost, a prisoner in a world that, awake or asleep, I had never dreamed of. Was there the smallest hope that a passing ship might rescue me? A remote chance, since the island was far to the west of the lane taken by our caravels, or so Captain Roa had said at the first signs of the hurricane. Could I somehow build a canoe or a small boat that would take me eastward, an island at a time, to Hispaniola? A bleak prospect, since I lacked the tools and was not a carpenter.

The important fact was that, by some miracle, I still lived. But why, of all the caravel's men, had I been cast, apparently alone, upon this island? Was it purposeful or by chance? One or the other, it did not matter, I told myself, and as I did so the words spoken to the eleven disciples went through my mind:

"Go ye into all the world, and preach the gospel to every creature."

I had no way of knowing whether anyone lived upon the island or not. But just silently saying Christ's words lifted my spirits.

The stallion, his coat ashine with salt from the sea, raised his head and neighed, happy to be on land after the ordeal on the ship, content in the abundant grass. I climbed down off the rock, went to where he was grazing, and patted his black muzzle. I spoke to him affectionately in words I had heard Don Luis use.

The sun was now far down in the west. As I walked along the edge of the meadow, I happened upon the trunk of a tree, fallen many years before. It was a good ten strides in length, hollow for half its length, wide enough for me to crawl into, and tinder-dry. I would have preferred a modest hut with a palm-thatched roof, such as those on Isla del Oro, but the timber and palm fronds for the undertaking I lacked at the moment.

Satisfied that the hoary log was the best I could do for the night, and that I was fortunate to have it, I went in search of my supper.

I found a small opening in what seemed to be a solid wall of trees and, entering it for a short way, managed to collect some pieces of fruit. Each was somewhat larger than my fist, and when the green skin was peeled away a pale white core was revealed that melted in the mouth.

While I stood eating the last of my supper, I heard a soft rustling sound, the barest movement of leaves above my head. Looking upward toward the tops of the trees, where the last faint light of day still lingered, I met the downward gaze of eyes that were at once human and inhuman. The face staring down at me was the color of soot, of the deepest black, bordered beneath with an enormous red beard.

I had seen this animal before in the jungles of Isla del Oro. It was an araguato, or howling monkey, a long-limbed creature quick in its actions, making great leaps with ease, yet capable of sitting for hours without movement other than that of scratching itself or its neighbor.

The araguato presented no danger to me, but danger did lurk in the jungle, as I knew from my days on Isla del Oro. It came upon padded feet, swift and quick as the wind, in the shape of the black-spotted jaguar. There were snakes the size of a twig, the exact color of a leaf, whose bite left one dead within the hour.

And this was on my mind as I crawled into the hollow log and tried to make myself comfortable for the night. If the log had had a door, I would have closed and bolted it securely.

I was sinking into sleep when I felt something crawling along my legs. Not a snake, as I first thought, but

108

something with four feet. Thinking to win its favor, I lay still while it trod the length of my back, daintily stepped on my face, and quietly launched forth into the night. It proved to be a coatimundi, an omnivorous animal with a tail that was long and ringed, a shy and gentle creature that in time became my friend, but who, unlike the stallion, remained wild at heart. I gave him the name Valiente.

I awakened with the sun well launched in a deep blue sky. Scrambling out of my home, stiff in every joint, I stood facing the new day, my second day on the island.

The sea was calm, the mountainous coast clear against the far horizon. The stream made no sound as it wandered out of the jungle and lost itself in the tides of the estuary. Small waves slid in upon the beach. Gulls were circling in search of food.

Standing beside my log home, I looked out at the meadow ablaze in the morning light, at the vaulting sky without a cloud, and thought, This is the way the world must have looked on the first day of creation. This was the Garden, and I the first man to enter its gates.

On my knees I gave thanks to God for the day and for all the days to come, whatever they might bring. I resolved, kneeling there, that I would not live from one breath to the next, hoping to be rescued or planning to escape, as if I were a forlorn prisoner held by some evil power. I would not live in fear. I would shape my life with what things I possessed, as if I were to spend all the rest of it here, on a nameless island.

During the night the tides had strewn the shore with wreckage from the *Santa Margarita*. None of it could I use, except for some pieces of wood and one of my boots, which I had kicked off when I swam ashore. In my search I came upon a length of balsa, a very light wood much favored on the island of gold. It was large enough to support my weight, but of a shape that would tend to roll in the water, so I fastened pieces of timber on either side of it, like fins, using strands of kelp to bind them together.

With a makeshift paddle I set off for the wreck, marked only by the mainmast, hoping that I would find a piece of metal that I could fashion into some sort of ax. The Indians of Isla del Oro used obsidian to face their tools, but there was no sign of this flintlike stone anywhere on the shore.

The mast of the *Santa Margarita* had not moved. It thrust itself out of the water for a third of its length.

Wrapped around it was a sizable square of canvas, a part of the caravel's forward sail. I hauled it in after great effort, since it was water-soaked and I needed to take care not to upset my tipsy craft.

A heavy brass band encircled the top of the mast, but it was so embedded in the wood that it wouldn't budge. I found, however, a good length of rope trailing out just below the surface of the water, which I would be able to use to make a bridle for the stallion. The strip of canvas could be fashioned into a shirt, since mine was in tatters, should I be able to make myself a needle. The Indians of Isla del Oro used thorns and fish bones for this purpose and fiber for thread.

The water was as clear as air. The *Santa Margarita* lay upon a jagged reef, broken amidships, the fore part lying on its side, the stern and main deck sitting upright.

I expected to see many drowned men there among the wreckage, but I saw only three. Two sailors who grasped each other in a death grip were wedged between the ship's broken ribs. The third drowned man I recognized. It was Baltasar Guzmán. He lay at the foot of the companionway, apparently entangled in wreckage as he started to climb out of the hold. A gold nugget was clasped to his chest. Small, bright-colored fish swam in and out of his trailing beard.

I did not give up the thought that Don Luis had managed to save himself, for he was a fearless swimmer. Instead of swimming to the island as I had done, he could have gone north, to the coast that lay farther from the *Santa Margarita.*

I was keenly disappointed at having failed to salvage much that could be used. In the wreck were chests of salt meat, tools of every description, cordage, nails and iron straps, watertight kegs of powder, muskets, lances and swords with which to defend myself—all of use, all in water too deep for me to reach.

I felt better when, three days later, in the wake of a strong north wind, the *Santa Margarita*'s mast pointed straight toward heaven and then, as I watched from the beach, slowly sank from view. No longer would I be mocked by her presence.

For the first week I lived on clams that I gathered in the estuary, small ones the size of my little finger, using my bare feet to locate them. I was tired already of eating these delicacies raw as they came from the sea and thought longingly of how they would taste cooked with a rasher of bacon and paved with eggs. Bacon I did not possess, but eggs, turtle eggs by the dozen, were to be found along the shore. What I really lacked was fire.

Recalling from my days on Isla del Oro that fire could be made by twirling the point of a stick in a soft, dry piece of wood, I spent an afternoon gathering materials.

A suitable stick I found on the beach. The dry wood and tinder were harder to come by, all the wood along the beach and around the edge of the jungle being soaked with ocean and rain. But I managed to collect a handful of dustlike particles from inside my hollow log, which I carefully arranged in a cupped rock, as I had seen it done on the island, placed my pointed stick in the midst of the pieces, and began to move it rapidly back and forth between my palms.

The twirling went on for the better part of an hour, the pile of scrapings steadily diminishing, until at last, as dusk came, it disappeared, having yielded not a single spark, let alone living fire.

This failure discouraged me completely, to the point that for one whole day I sat near my log more or less staring at the ground. I did have enough energy, however, with some effort, to go into the jungle and gather fruit for my supper.

While there I encountered an animal that the Indians on Isla del Oro called a "hay" and I later learned was a tree sloth. The cacique's youngest son had one of these animals as a pet, and it had amused me to watch it climb down from its perch to be fed, taking half an hour to go three feet.

This one was not feeding but hanging upside down, holding on to a branch with its three-toed feet. It kept blinking its eyes at me while I gathered fruit, as though it recognized me as a friend, perhaps a cousin.

For my supper, in addition to the fruit, I had heaping handfuls of berries that I found in the meadow on the way home. They were the size of my thumb, blue in color, and, though well seeded, had a sweet, melting flavor that surprised the tongue. These, the coatimundi liked.

The heat was more intense than usual, so instead of crawling into my log, I made a pallet of leaves outside the opening. As I lay there, a soft glow came into the western sky, which I took to be the moon. But when time went by and it failed to change its position in the heavens, I decided that the glow must come from the volcano I had sighted nine days before, my first day upon the island.

I had kept count of the time since leaving Seville, and because it was now the 29th of August, the feast day of St. John the Baptist, I gave the volcano his illustrious name. I said it aloud, and as the name rolled across the meadow, it occurred to me that the glow must come from hot lava and that I could go there and bring back a few embers to start my own fire. Once it was started, I would tend it carefully.

With this thought in mind, I settled down to sleep, calming my stomach by thoughts of a bowl filled with cold cucumbers shredded fine, bread crumbs, a generous helping of oil from Ubeda, vinegar, and water fresh from the stream—a bowl of *gazpacho*. I also pictured a plate of calves' feet, and if not them, a cow's head, however tough it might be.

I must have fallen asleep, but not for long, for when I opened my eyes a pack of small animals had taken up a position not more than twenty paces away. They were squatting bunched together in a half-circle. In the glow of the volcano their eyes glittered like mica, and sounds issued from their mouths, small grunts and a chattering of teeth, as if they were talking to each other.

I jumped to my feet and threw a length of tree limb in their direction. They instantly disappeared, but when I lay down again they were back, sitting in a half-circle, closer this time, so close that I could make out that they were a species of dog, the same animal I had seen on Isla del Oro, which hunted in packs and was captured, fattened, and eaten by the Indians. Their heads were round as a ball, their large eyes bulged, but their peculiar characteristic was that they were pink-skinned and scanty of hair.

The little pink dogs went on chattering to themselves. Close to me now, they gave off a strong, sickening odor, as if they had recently gorged themselves on carrion. They chattered until the moon rose, then quietly trotted away through the grass and disappeared.

I fell asleep, determined, as I thought of the sloth hanging upside down in the jungle, blinking its eyes at me in a fraternal way, of the sloth on Isla del Oro who moved when it did move at the pace of a foot an hour, determined somehow to make a fire. Besides furnishing edible food, the flames would afford me a small measure of protection.

But first I would attend to the stallion. Then to the building of a hut, since each morning I crawled out of the log more tired than when I had crawled into it.

•
•

I was not a horseman. I had never been astride the stallion, but I knew from the riding I had done, most of it
on the broad back of a donkey, and from watching Don
Luis, how a good horseman should hold the reins,
handle the bit, how to put spurs to the animal's flank
and when. I lacked everything—spurs, bridle, a bit, a
saddle—but all of them I would somehow contrive.

I cut the rope I had salvaged from the wreck and used
as a tether, and tied it in such a way that it fitted snugly
around Bravo's muzzle. To this headstall I fastened two
lengths of rope to serve as reins. The result was crude
and somewhat of a surprise to the stallion, who, used to
the best of harness, winced and shied away when I tried
to slip it over his head. He gave me a dark glance from
his rolling eyes that made me feel that I did not know
what I was up to. Accustomed to Don Luis' arrogant
commands and sharp spurs, he took me at once for
someone he could bully. I liked Bravo and admired his
beauty, but this was not enough. I had to win his respect. More than that, I had to win it by showing him
who was the master.

I collected a bundle of moss from the jungle to serve
as saddle, thinking to stuff it into a sack. But the thorns
I was forced to use to bind the whole together proved

bothersome, so I gave up the idea of a saddle and decided to ride the stallion bareback.

By evening, having labored since noon, I was ready to make the attempt. I led Bravo to my log and climbed upon it. I spoke to him softly, repeating words that I had heard Don Luis use. Words such as *"hombre"* and *"amigo"* and blandishments like *"Mira, señor el león bravo* (Look, sir, brave lion)."

I eased myself onto the stallion's back, holding the reins in one hand as I had seen it done before. He didn't rear up on his hind legs, but he did make two leaps, the second of which sent me sprawling in the grass. I tried again, this time remaining on his back for three short leaps.

The meadow was strewn with gray rocks thrown there, I presumed, by the volcano. Fearing a cracked head, I led the stallion to the beach, where the sand proved softer to fall upon. I gave up the idea of trying to control him by gripping the reins. Instead, I grasped his long, thick mane and hung on, letting him take me where he willed. Thus I labored until nightfall.

The next morning I was too stiff to ride, but in the afternoon I braved the ordeal again. By dusk I had learned to stay on the stallion's back without clutching his mane. At the end of the week I could control him with the reins except when he got it into his head to stand on his hind legs or kick up his heels. At these times I closed my eyes and hung on.

I had plenty of time to perfect my horsemanship, so at once I began the construction of a hut. It didn't prove as difficult as I thought it would be, for near the shore was a large pile of lava, made up of rocks of various sizes, none too heavy for me to handle. I simply shifted them around to form an enclosure seven paces in length and five paces in width. The crevices between the rocks I filled with mud from the estuary.

This took me six days. I then set about the gathering of materials for a roof. The task would have been much easier if I had used the stallion as a pack horse. But he was such a magnificent animal that I couldn't bring myself to pile burdens on his back. As it was, I piled them on my own back and carried branches and palm fronds from the jungle, withes from the mangroves at the head of the estuary, and mud to bind them together.

This task wasn't easy, because I had little knowledge of how even a simple house should be built, though I had lived in one all of my life. But in the end, after two hard weeks of toil, I owned a dwelling that—while it lacked windows, had only an opening for a door, a roof that was too low and on which the thatch would probably leak—still promised more comfort than my hollow log.

At dawn, after the first night in my new home, I set about the making of a pair of boots. The little amount of walking I had done had left me with tender feet, too tender for me to attempt a long barefoot walk to the volcano, which I judged to be distant some two or three leagues. It would have been much better had I been able to ride the stallion, but the jungle was so dense that such a journey was impossible.

The boot I had recovered on the beach was shrunken out of shape, but it furnished me with enough leather for two thick soles. These I cut out in a crude pattern to suit my feet, beating the leather with rock against rock, using sand and the sharp edges of many seashells.

It took me two days to make the soles, three days to cut out part of the canvas I had retrieved from the wreck. At the end of a week I owned a pair of boots with open toes and heels and cloth tops that also served as leggings—not pinked cordovan, I must say. I also made myself a rough shirt out of what was left of the sail, a sleeveless poncho without a collar, using thorns to pin it together.

The next morning, in my new boots and shirt, with a conch shell, from the beach, that was large enough to carry a good quantity of coals, I set off.

The plume of feathery smoke that rose from the volcano gave me a sighting. Wherever I might be along the way, it would be my guide. I took no food, thinking to gather fruit when hungry, and no water, since there was nothing to carry it in.

It was very hot, steaming and cloudless, though the day had just begun, with the result that, before I had gone half a league up a steep slope, through trees and heavy brush, I was forced to stop for breath.

Farther along I came to a stream and, resting on its bank, counted many troutlets lying on the bottom among the stones. Trees heavy with fruit grew everywhere, and bushes hung thick with black and red berries. I took note of this sylvan place as a future source of food.

Following the stream, I entered a cathedral-like grove. The trees, which were of a variety I'd never seen before, had delicate, transparent leaves the shape of coins, fastened to branches at such an angle that, as I passed among them and stirred the air, they seemed to turn full circle on their stems.

A heavy odor of many fragrances surrounded me as I moved along—of flowers blooming somewhere out of sight, of leaves and moss wet from rain, and the lingering smell of some sweet bush. Far above me through rents in the foliage, I caught glimpses of the sky, a startling blue, since I was traveling in emerald shadow.

Orchids grew everywhere, and butterflies that looked like orchids danced in the green twilight. A flock of friendly parrots followed for a while, flying from tree to tree, waiting for me to pass, then flying on ahead to wait until I passed again, shrieking all the while. Brightbilled toucans, holding in their claws the same kind of fruit I often had for supper, stopped eating to watch me. In the near distance a waterfall came into view, the stream leaping wildly out as if to free itself from the earth.

The beauty of the falling water, the arching trees, the bright-colored birds, and the living breath of the world that lay about me slowed my footsteps. Casting my eyes upward in thanks to my Maker for this great gift of beauty, I failed to see a stone hidden in the grass, fell headlong upon the earth, and for a moment stayed prone and breathless, thinking, This has happened to me before.

I soon realized that it had not happened to me at all, but to another, and that I had read about it in a history book. It was Scipio, the Roman general, who, upon reaching Africa, stumbled as he leaped ashore. His soldiers took the accident as an omen of evil. But Scipio, clasping the earth, cried out, "Thou canst not escape me, Africa. I hold thee tight between my arms."

Not clasping the earth, feeling foolish, I picked myself up and went on, at sundown reaching a treeless savannah covered with thorn bushes and strewn with rocks. The thorns on the intertwined bushes were sharp as needles, long as a finger, the same kind of thorn with which I had fastened my poncho.

From this open place I had a good view of St. John the Baptist, and I was delighted to see that I had not wandered off the path I had chosen. The gray plume spread out to westward, moved by a wind that did not blow here on the savannah. Through the falling night I could see a ring of fire just below the summit and from it a fiery rivulet flowing downward.

In the dusk I came unexpectedly upon a barrier of tumbled lava that I soon discovered marked the edge of a deep and heavily forested ravine. From its distant bottom the sound of rushing water reached my ears. I had gone as far that day as I could go.

Near the edge of the ravine I found a flat rock and made a bed upon it, high off the ground. While offering me a secure place to spend the night, it unfortunately was surrounded by trees.

I had no sooner stretched myself out on my hard bed than I heard a stirring far above me. The stirring became a murmurous, drawn-out sound, like wind rising. Then there fell from above a short silence, broken abruptly by a single cry that was soft and almost human. The cry changed to a long, inhuman shriek, and again there was a short period of silence.

Suddenly, a congregation of voices broke forth from the treetops. A hundred, a thousand, anguished fiends in the halls of hell could not have made a mightier roar. It shook the trees around me, the very rock where I lay. My discomfort, as the sound of the howling monkeys beat down upon my ears, was not lessened by the thought that I had neglected, while I'd had the chance, to gather fruit for my supper.

Before the sun rose, I was on my way into the wooded ravine, where I struggled downward for hours before I reached the stream. I followed the stream, which trended toward the volcano and rose, I believed, somewhere on its slopes.

I passed its source, which I named Dos Manantiales,

for two large springs that flowed from a rocky cavern. I left the trees and climbed steeply through barren fields strewn with ash and pitted boulders.

I had climbed only a third of the distance or less to the mouth of the volcano, but already the earth felt hot beneath my feet, and on my tongue was the coppery taste of smoke. Deciding that it would be dangerous to travel farther, I set off to explore the country that lay immediately around me.

Leafless trees and stumps of various sizes that looked like black fangs were scattered over the slope, evidence that the volcano had erupted at times in the past. A wisp of smoke rose from one of the stumps, and upon examination I found deep inside it a core of living coals. These I scooped up in the conch shell, wrapped the shell in grass, and at a trot started off down the mountain.

From this height I was able to see my broad meadow, the white beach, and the reef running out into the channel where the *Santa Margarita* lay. Then northward for a league or two stretched a blue jungle without any sign of habitation. But just beyond the jungle I made out what seemed to be a number of towers grouped together along a curving arm of the sea. The wind had changed, sending clouds of smoke swirling around me, so I could not be certain of what I saw. The towers, I decided, could be something I had conjured up.

I went downward, faster than I had ascended, but often stopped to blow the coals alive. I kept an eye out for dry twigs and, finding none when an hour passed and the fire grew faint, I hammered a piece from my poncho, using rocks, rolled the cloth tight, and placed it among the coals. Repeating this procedure from time to time, though I found no dry twigs, I managed to keep the fire alive while I struggled in and out of the deep ravine and came at last within half a league of home.

Threatening clouds had built up steadily since noonday, and as I neared the meadow a driving rain overtook me. I slipped out of my poncho, covered the conch shell, and ran for home, crossing the stream in one long leap.

Inside the hut I unwrapped the conch shell—first my poncho, then the layer of grass—and shook the coals out on the earth floor, using great care with them. They looked pale and dead. I stirred them carefully with my finger, but still they appeared dead.

Getting down on my knees, I blew gently upon the lifeless dust, all that remained of the coals I had taken from the volcano. Suddenly, a spark leaped out of the gray mass, making a small sound. A second spark crackled and flew away. I hurriedly stripped a dry palm leaf from the roof over my head, placed it among the coals, and gently blew again. The leaf curled and crackled and to my great delight burst into flame.

I had nothing to cook that night, but I did have a fire. Sitting beside it, eating fruit and berries, I regaled myself with thoughts of the food I would cook in the days to come. In the meantime, I also thought of breasts of pigeon garnished with cream and flour. Of black Ubeda olives swimming in oil, and ham hocks not too lean for tasting.

The rain drummed on the thatch. Here and there, water dripped through and made pools on the floor, but still I was snug. Valiente, the coatimundi, curled contentedly beside the fire, perhaps the first he had ever seen.

Before I lay down for the night, I gathered up odds and ends left over from building and put them on the burning logs. I fell asleep with fire shadows dancing merrily on the roof and the sound of the rain.

Exhausted from my long journey, I slept late, until the sun shone hot through the opening. I awakened hungry, with thoughts of food, of cooked clams and a fish, should I be able to snare one among the tide pools. But first I would go to the beach and gather driftwood for the fire.

I glanced across the room and saw to my dismay that the fire had died. Ends of palm fronds lay in a circle around a bed of gray coals. Jumping to my feet, I blew upon the ashes. I stirred them with a stick and blew again. But to no avail. The fire that I had brought home from the volcano, after an arduous journey, had died while I dreamed of a roasted haunch and skewered ham from the grape-fed pigs of Jerez.

In a chastened mood, after a meager breakfast of berries, I went along the beach, as was my habit, in search of flotsam left by the tides that had come and gone during the night.

I found two pieces of timber from the *Santa Margarita,* sound wood but of no value, since I had given up all thought of building a raft. I also found two large kegs marked *pólvora,* the letters burned deep into the oak. The gunpowder would be dry, for the kegs were tight and sealed with wax. Although I could foresee no need for powder, lacking as I did a weapon with which to use it, I rolled the kegs high on the shore beyond the reach of the tide.

At the northernmost part of the cove, wedged between two rocks and wound about by kelp, I came upon the body of a man. The bones had been picked clean by creatures of the sea, except for the legs, which were encased in tight cordovan boots.

It could have been the skeleton of one of Don Luis' retainers, possibly the barber, for he had worn boots of a similar style. It was not that of Don Luis, however, it being too tall in stature.

I buried the skeleton in the sand and, kneeling, again said a prayer for the salvation of the souls of all the men who had gone down with the *Santa Margarita.* And for the Indians of Isla del Oro.

I had not been in this part of the meadow before, a longbow shot from the flat rock. It was a place where a small grove of trees stood isolated from the edge of the jungle, the trees bound together in a dense thicket of pendulous vines covered with thorns.

As I passed the grove, by chance the sun glittered on a curiously shaped stone which caught my eye. Looking closer, I saw that it marked a narrow path leading from the meadow into the heart of a woody thicket.

This path I followed, mindful of the thorns, and soon came upon a clearing, triangular in shape and some twenty paces from base to apex. At the far end of the triangle there stood a stone figure twice my height, of such a ferocious mien that the blood ran chill in my veins.

The figure was twice as large as the one I had seen on the island of gold and of a rougher stone, painted in bright colors. The head bore a crown of fruit inter-twined with leaves and what looked to be some form of flying monster, small yet enormous-eyed, with many sets of wings, one set folded in upon the other.

The shock I had felt on Isla del Oro was nothing to what I now felt. I stood rooted to the earth, unable to move.

Beneath the elaborate headdress was the face of a woman. The broad cheeks were scarified, cut crosswise with delicate slashes, as was the chin. Naked to the waist, with four hanging breasts, she bore upon her shoulders and arms the coils of writhing snakes whose heads she cradled in her hands.

It was the feet, however, that held my gaze. They

were bare under the folds of a dress that was adorned with flowers of many colors. The toes were long and grasped the earth. They were not toes but talons, hooked and pointed, dripping with blood.

In horror, I stepped back. "God!" I cried out to the sky. "Oh, God in heaven!"

Carefully placed in the grass in a circle around the stone image were what I took to be offerings—a bundle of the fruit I often ate, baskets of nuts and berries, and a scattering of cacao seeds and flowers.

Someone had put them there at the feet of the goddess. And within the last day, for everything was freshly gathered. The island was not deserted. I was not alone. Not alone!

I looked around for footprints and found none, but in back of the stone image there was a well-worn path that led away from the clearing and grove of trees, northward into the jungle.

I followed it for a way and then returned to the clearing, drawn back by the serpent goddess. The sun was higher now and shone upon her, revealing things about the face that I had not seen before. The eyes were heavy-lidded and nearly closed. Yet, as I stood there, her gaze sought mine and held it. The stone lips were parted, as if she were about to speak to me.

Against my will, I listened for her words. What would they be? Why did this monstrous image hold me there at her feet, fascinated and trembling?

I waited, unable to move. The sun rose higher. Now I saw a half-smile on her parted lips. The serpents on her arms seemed alive, the scales glistening as they uncoiled. With great effort, I wrested myself free and, stumbling, fled through the thicket. I ran until I reached the sea. I walked the shore while the waves came in, and in time got my thoughts in order.

I had come to New Spain to bring Christ's message to those who had never heard it. On Isla del Oro, my efforts had failed, but now there was another chance for me. The island, as I had observed from the volcano, was large, much larger than the island of gold, and though I had not seen a single native or even his footprints, still there must be upon it habitations and villages, perhaps a city.

I had lived on the island for more than a month. In this time I had done little except think of my own comforts. I had found shelter. I had gathered food and regretted that I didn't have more and of a different kind. I had found fire on the mountain and then slothfully lost it. I had said prayers morning and night, but by rote.

What made the past days even more barren was that since boyhood I had admired and tried to emulate in small ways the life of St. Francis of Assisi. He who slept upon the ground, ate dry crusts, and when a thief took his coat and ran away, ran after the man and insisted that he take his trousers, too.

Humbled, with the two pieces of timber, binding them together with seaweed, I made a cross, which I set on the headland. I knelt before it and at dusk returned and sang the Salve Regina to the homing gulls and my beautiful stallion and mischievous coatimundi, to all things God had made, the world that lay about me.

•

———

That night the monkeys returned and roared until the moon had set. At this time, in the deep silence that followed their horrendous cries, I heard a sound, a faint stirring softly repeated. At first I thought it came from the waves on the shore. Then it sounded to me more like the stallion moving about as he grazed in the meadow.

At dawn when I went outside, my eyes fell at once upon a series of footprints marked clearly in the grass. The prints were small, possibly left by a very young boy.

I recalled that the natives of Isla del Oro were small, the tallest scarcely reaching to my chest. The natives on this island—and there was at least one—were probably small, too. But I doubted the tracks left there during the night were those of a man.

Whoever made them had approached within a dozen paces of where I lay, unsuspecting. Had this person come to do me harm? Had he spied upon me from afar as I went about my daily rounds? Was he spying upon me now, at this moment? These thoughts were unsettling.

Valiente was of no use as a watchman, for he usually spent his nights abroad. So I gathered green creepers in the jungle and braided them into a clumsy rope with which, before I went to bed, I tethered the stallion near

132

the hut, thinking that he would raise an alarm should someone approach. This was small comfort, since I had no weapon. But to be forewarned of an attack, I reasoned, was better than to be killed while I slept.

I stayed awake most of the night, kept company by the howling monkeys, but I heard no unfamiliar sounds. Bravo was grazing peacefully at dawn when I fell asleep, to dream of pots of steaming food and snow-cooled milk. I awakened to the smell of smoke.

Looking out, I saw, to my great surprise, a shallow pit surrounded by a neat pile of stones, not ten paces from the hut. In the center of the pit burned a lively fire.

I ran outside, scarcely trusting my eyes. But the fire was real. It burned my hand. No one was in sight. I found no footprints in the grass. Raising my voice, I shouted, *"Hola, amigo, hola!"* I shouted the greeting over and over, but received no answer.

On a flat stone beside the fire was a length of cotton fishing line and a hook made of gold. Yes, gold. Only a friend would have built a fire for me. Only someone who wished me well would have left me the means by which to feed myself. The gold hook meant that the metal was common on the island. But who was this Indian friend who watched over me? Boy or man, why did he come to the camp by stealth in the night and flee with the dawn?

I lost no time getting to the beach. With my new line and the golden hook baited with clams, I cast out into the estuary. Losing more than I landed, because the hook was barbless, I still caught two silver-sided fish, each of a good size, which I cleaned and split.

I went to the shore again and brought back driftwood for two days' burning. I built up the fire, made a fine bed of glowing coals, and grilled my catch. Though I lacked soup and vegetables and a cool beverage, it was the best meal I had tasted in many long months.

That night, determined to learn who my visitor was, I built up the fire and slept near the open door of my hut. It was stormy, with waves crashing upon the shore and wind whipping the tall grass in the meadow. The horde of little dogs appeared and sat beside the fire, chattering away for an hour or so.

The wind died toward morning. In the silence, I heard someone moving around beyond the ring of fire-light. I got up and stealthily circled the meadow, stopping now and then to listen for sounds in the tall grass.

I heard nothing as I moved, but at dawn I found beside the fire a stout hardwood club. It was longer than my arm and faced at the larger end with a sharp flake of obsidian. It could be used as either a weapon or a cutting tool. Beside it lay a bowl of fruit, several strands of fiber, and a needle made of a fish bone.

My friend, whoever it was, must have watched me while I struggled to cut cloth with the honed edge of a clamshell. He must have seen me trying to make the poncho, piecing it together with a handful of thorns.

I discovered fresh footprints on the beach, but all of them belonged to the same person. It was puzzling that only one Indian came to my camp. Could there be only one living in the jungle? Or did he live in a nearby village, for some reason keeping my presence a secret from all others in the tribe?

The bowl held several kinds of fruit. Especially good was a small green melon with orange-colored flesh that melted softly in the mouth, leaving a taste of custard seasoned with spice. As I ate it, I cast about in my mind for some small gift I could leave by the fire in return for the gifts left for me.

Something. Anything. Alas, I was as poor as a mouse that lives in a village church. But gift or not, I wouldn't rest until I had discovered the identity of my elusive visitor and friend.

Now that I felt safe, with a handy weapon at my side and a fire burning, I decided to sleep in the open, for the nights were hot. I made a bed of meadow grass against the front of the hut and lay down as soon as it grew dark, thinking to get my sleep before the hour when the visitor might appear.

I awoke after midnight, judging by the position of the stars. As I lay in the open, encircled by the black jungle, I thought of my books, those I'd had to leave at home as well as those, the Canticles of St. Francis and the Bible, that were lying beneath the waters. I knew my books almost by heart, but it was always a happy moment when I took them up and turned the pages and saw the words again. It was like meeting friends you have not seen for a long time.

A half-moon rose above the trees. From far off came the soft rumble of the volcano. A reddish light shone on the water; I presumed it to be a reflection of its fire.

The stars that wheeled toward the dawn also looked down on the stone idol, who stood with her bloody talons gripping the same earth I lay upon. She had haunted me since the moment when I had fled the clearing. Soon, this very day, I must go back to the jungle and stand in front of her. I must meet her half-closed eyes and stony gaze and face her down.

Toward daylight I dozed but suddenly awakened to the sound of Bravo neighing. Cautiously, I got to my feet, taking care to stand in the shadow of the doorway.

Light began to show in the east and on the highest branches of the trees. Beyond the fire and the circle where the stallion grazed, at the very edge of the jungle, I saw a figure. It stood for a moment looking in my direction, then, no more than a moving shadow, crossed the meadow in the direction of the beach.

It was possible that there were two Indians, even more, who visited the camp. I waited, standing in the shadows. The lone figure disappeared from view.

Now was the moment to follow and call out a greeting. I hesitated, thinking that the visitor planned to return, possibly with a gift. Then would be the time to step forth quietly, to speak, to give my thanks.

The eastern sky had grown light. There was no sign of the visitor. I started for the shore without delay. I found it deserted, but in the wet sand were fresh prints. I followed them to the far end of the cove, where they moved about in a circle, then turned away from the shore.

Here, I lost them in the grass. I stood for a while, undecided about what to do. I had an odd feeling that whoever it might be was not far away, perhaps hidden at the edge of the jungle, watching. As I stood there, gazing in all directions, I felt somewhat like a fool.

After a moment it occurred to me to follow the path I had taken four mornings before. I went quietly. When I reached the grove of trees and thorn bushes. I paused to listen. I heard nothing except a pair of macaws chattering in a tree.

I made my way through the thorns, taking one careful

step at a time. I reached the triangular clearing in front of the image. The evil place was still in darkness, save for a glimmer of light on the winged monster that adorned the head of the goddess.

With the rising sun the light descended, revealing the stone face, the slashes across cheeks and chin, the half-closed eyes. I crossed myself and met her gaze. I did not move from where I stood.

I became aware of the strong, not unpleasant odor of burning copal, which I had encountered on the island of gold. It rose in wisps of resinous smoke from a bowl that someone had placed at the foot of the goddess.

I had thought I was alone. But as the light grew, I made out a figure lying prone, arms outstretched, before the stone image. The figure was clothed in a scarlet huipal. It was the same person, man or boy, I had seen in the meadow. The worshiper lay motionless, but I heard a few faint words, the same words said slowly over and over.

It must have been my labored breathing, for I did not move or speak. Suddenly the worshiper arose and, with a cry of surprise, turned to face me.

It was neither a man nor a boy who stood there before me, but a girl, no older than my young sister. Her hair was glossy black, reaching to her waist. She grasped it in both hands, whether in alarm or surprise, I cannot say.

The next moment, without a word spoken, she was gone. Not by the way I had come, but by a different, a secret way, perhaps, toward the south and the volcano, on a path that led into the deepest heart of the jungle.

The girl was gone so suddenly that I had no chance to utter more than one feeble word of greeting.

I ran along the path she had taken, past the stone image to the far end of the clearing and the edge of the jungle. There I halted and, cupping my hands, shouted a word I had learned on Isla del Oro, an Indian salutation. I shouted it with all the breath I could summon. There was no reply.

The path led into a tangle of trees, thorns, and looping vines so dense that, after a half-dozen steps, I gave up my pursuit and turned back. Yet the girl had made her way into this jungle and, without a sound, had swiftly disappeared. Who was she? Where was her home? Why had she come in the dark to bring me gifts? Why had she fled?

These questions and many others I pondered.

There was little doubt that the girl lived close by and, considering her age, which I took to be thirteen or fourteen, with her mother and father. On her way to the beach to fish or gather clams, she had seen me in the meadow, a tall, white-skinned stranger. She had seen the stallion. She had marveled at both, but she had kept these marvels a secret. For what reason I didn't know, except that my sister loved secrets and often made them up when they didn't really exist.

Watching me as I went about the meadow, when I traveled to the volcano and came back with a shell full of ashes, seeing that I ate nothing but fruit, that I had to pin my shirt together with thorns, she had taken pity on me.

I slept outside that night, as I had before, with a good fire burning, but apparently she didn't return. If she did so during the brief times I dozed, she left no gifts.

Nor did she return the following night, though I kept a wakeful watch. Toward dawn of the third night after our encounter, with a half-moon shining in my eyes, I awakened to see a figure as it left the fire and started away. It looked to be larger than the girl, but this proved only a trick of the moonlight.

I jumped to my feet, not pausing to see if she had left another gift. Determined to catch the girl before she reached the jungle, I wasted no breath on an idle greeting.

She ran with her black hair streaming, not awkwardly with flailing arms as my sister ran, but gracefully, like a forest animal.

Before she reached the stream, I had gained a few steps on her. I lost them when she came to a boulder and had to make a circle while boldly I leaped over it but stumbled as I landed. In the tall grass I gained back what I'd lost.

At the very edge of the jungle, just as she was about to disappear from sight, I overtook the girl. I grasped her arm lightly, too lightly, for she pulled away and the next moment would have faded off into the trees had I not taken hold of her with both hands.

It had been a game she was playing with me. Now the game was over and she was in the grasp of a stranger she had seen only from a distance. She hid her face against her shoulder. I could feel her trembling.

"Señorita," I said, though out of breath and knowing that she wouldn't understand one word of what I was about to say, "I only wish to thank you for all you have given me."

No words ever fell upon less comprehending ears.

The Spanish tongue possesses many beautiful sounds—I wouldn't set myself up as a judge, since I have a knowledge of only three other languages, French and Latin and Italian—the most beautiful sounds I think in all the world. But—I might have been speaking with my mouth full of pebbles. The girl tried to cover her ears. She squirmed to get free.

I dared not let go lest she disappear. Yet what had I gained by running her down, standing there with a firm grip on her shoulders, speaking words that she not only didn't understand but whose sound actually pained her?

I let go my hold and stepped back.

She looked up at me in surprise, settling her dress around her shoulders. She had black eyes and high cheekbones. In each ear she wore a small gold plug. On the point of her chin was a single blue dot. She was what I would call a comely girl, and seemed to know it.

To express my thanks, I waved toward the fire, in pantomime carefully threaded a needle, and went

142

through the act of sewing. I pretended to eat a piece of fruit that dripped juice. I then took a step backward and made a low bow, placing my hands on my chest, as is the custom when addressing a queen.

As I straightened up after this elaborate mimicry, the girl was no longer there. She had fled without a sound through the tall grass into the fastness of the jungle. I listened and heard nothing. I waited, thinking that now she was free, she might venture back. I waited a long time, until the sun rose on the new day.

Disappointed at the turn events had taken, I walked to the shore to catch my breakfast. The tide was out and the fish were not biting, so I gathered clams on the beach. Being in no mood to trudge back to my hut, I sat on the sand and ate them raw.

I felt foolish when I thought of how I had lamely struggled through the dumb show of thanking the girl for her gifts. Languages were easy for me. I could learn in time to speak her tongue well.

It was possible that she had circled back by her secret path and was now in the clearing. She apparently went there every morning to burn copal and prostrate herself before the stone image. With the prospect of meeting the girl for the second time that morning, I started off for the jungle clearing.

I approached it with care, so silently that the macaws never paused in their chattering, and a bright-banded coral snake, whose bite could bring death within the hour, never moved as I passed by.

I smelled the sweet odor of copal and saw its blue smoke drifting high among the trees. The clearing was deserted, but someone had been there that morning, for the bowl that held the incense was nearly full.

The goddess had not changed. The eyes were still half-closed; they still looked down upon me with a stony gaze that was at once piercing and slumberous. Upon the protruding lips was the beginning or the ending of a smile that, as before, both repelled and attracted me.

The serpents entwined about her I hadn't taken full note of until now. There were seven of them, all with many delicate scales that seemed to move as they caught the light, all with eyes that repeated the piercing, slumberous look of the goddess.

The smell of copal made my head reel. I took a step away and glanced up at the pure blue of the sky.

How could this Indian girl, a child, visit such a place, apparently every day, to worship the monstrous image, to lie prone before it and its writhing serpents, to bring offerings of fruit, to burn sweet-smelling copal? How? I asked myself. And what, what could she ever receive in return for such devotion?

Late that afternoon the girl walked out of the jungle, carrying a sheaf of green shoots, and went to where the stallion was grazing. She passed me without a glance as I sat in front of the hut, repairing my shirt with the newly acquired needle and thread.

Since he was not on a tether, I expected Bravo to bolt as she held out her hand. Instead, he allowed her to touch his muzzle, and when she offered him a handful of shoots he took them, switching his tail to show his thanks.

I had a sudden suspicion. It was Bravo she was curious and concerned about rather than me. The presents she had brought—the fruit, the weapon, the sewing things, the fire—all were bribes, means by which she had worked herself into my good graces and thus in a roundabout way into those of Bravo.

Proceeding with my task, I paid no attention to her. When I had finished with my shirt, she wandered over to where I sat. She still was barefooted but had braided her hair and set it on top of her head like a crown, which made her look older than she was.

Saying a few strange-sounding words but not to me especially, she glanced around at the meadow and sky, at last in my direction, and smiled stiffly. Then she walked away, taking her time, paused to touch the stallion's flank, waded the stream, and was gone, leaving behind her the sweet smell of burning copal.

The smell brought back the morning, the moments when I had stood in front of the stone goddess and wondered how the girl could possibly worship such a monstrous image.

I laid the needle and thread away and started to put on my mended shirt. The smell of copal still clung to it, so I went to the stream and spread it out on a flat rock. As I washed it with the clear-running water, I made a resolve. When the girl came again, as she surely would, I'd take her to the headland. There, by the wide sea, under the open sky, before the cross, I would set her feet upon the Christian path.

It would be hard to do, since our languages were so different. But with patience, in time, I would overcome the difficulties. Hers would be the first savage soul I had helped to save. God willing, there would be more!

She returned the next morning, bringing the stallion a basket of fruit, which he disdained, and from afar cast upon me one brief glance and left. It was the horse that fascinated her.

She came back in the afternoon, while I was at work on Bravo's halter, this time with a bundle of palm shoots balanced on her head. When he had eaten them, she wandered over to me, walking gracefully with her head high, as if she were still carrying the bundle of palm shoots. I noticed, however, that, as she walked, she was a little pigeon-toed.

She pointed to the stallion and by graceful signs made me see that she wished to climb on his back.

It was then that I had what seemed to be an ingenious idea. She could mount the stallion, I let her know, but first she must do something for me. Without a word being spoken, we struck a bargain.

I put my work away and walked with her to the shore, and together we climbed to the top of the headland, to the great flat stone where the cross stood. I knelt and asked her to kneel beside me. The sun cast a golden light across the waters. The girl smiled, but it was a puzzled smile, as well it might have been.

Around my neck was a chain with a medal showing the figure of Christ on the cross, the only possession of mine that had survived the wreck. I took it off and put it in her hand; then I pointed to the cross I had built.

She still looked puzzled. She wrinkled her brows and glanced from the figure in her hand to the wooden cross, but made no connection between them.

"This is Christ," I said, pointing to the figure on the medal. "This is Christ also," I said and again pointed to the wooden cross.

She helplessly shook her head and turned away from me and said something in her outlandish-sounding tongue. I couldn't even guess at the meaning of her words, but their tone was clear.

Suddenly I realized that what I was trying to do was doomed to failure. I was asking a little savage, an ignorant girl, at least one who was untutored, to understand, by the use of a few simple gestures and by words she had never heard before, an idea, a concept that was often difficult even for those who were schooled.

I was being a fool.

Embarrassed, I took the chain, put it around my neck, and got to my feet. I would have apologized had I had the words, even one word.

But I recovered myself enough to sing a tuneful song about the Virgin and was pleased to observe that the girl listened to me. More than that, she uttered words which I took to be praiseful, and by a movement of her hands showed that she wished to hear me sing again.

But these simple acts made me realize more than ever what could be understood between us and what not understood and not done. I wanted to bring Christ's message to the Indian girl and to those of her tribe who might come within the reach of my voice. The only way I could hope to accomplish this was by learning the language she used, whatever it might be.

I did learn her name. It was Ceela.

Ceela held me to my bargain. No sooner had we come down from the headland than she ran to where Bravo was grazing. She grasped his long mane and made a leap for his back, but he tossed his head and shied away. After I had brought him around again, I made a step with my hands and boosted her up. She took the reins, and off we went through the meadow, with me holding tight to the tether rope.

Arabian stallions are gentle and affectionate, much gentler than ordinary stallions. True to the breed, Bravo acted as if he and the girl were old friends. I don't know what Ceela felt, except that she sat smiling, with her skirts pulled up to her skinny knees, and held the reins like a proper horsewoman.

As for me, I nearly walked my legs off, but improved the time by taking a first lesson in what Ceela called Maya. I pointed to a rock and asked her for the word that meant rock in her language. We walked along the beach and I pointed out the sea, the waves, the shells, the gulls flying overhead. By nightfall I had accumulated thirty words, taking the second step toward learning the language of those who lived on the island.

Ceela came back the next afternoon and rode until dusk, with me walking beside her as before, again pointing at objects and learning their names.

The Mayan language, I had found in two long lessons, was difficult. Unlike the other languages I knew, it was not based upon Latin but upon rules and sounds of its own. Thus, *cenote,* as I was to learn when I saw it written down by Spanish priests, the word for waterhole, was pronounced with a hard *c.* The *X* in Xul, the word for the sixth month of the Mayan year, was given the sound of *sh*; and Xux, the morning star, Venus, was pronounced *shush.*

I asked Ceela for the word that meant horse. It was a joke, of course, but she thought seriously and finally gave me a long string of words that I didn't understand. In return I told her that Bravo was a *caballo.* She tried to say the word, failed, made a face as if she had eaten something bitter, and with a shrug dismissed the whole idea. She made it clear that Maya was the only language worth speaking. I never again used a Spanish word with her.

When she was able to ride by herself, I walked along beside her instead of leading the stallion. After a week of this I decided to enlist her help in making a saddle that we both could use. She brought a deerskin, which we laid out on the floor of the hut and cut to fit Bravo's back. It had no pommel or cantle, but sewed together with an underlayer of cotton and feathers, a sort of fat pillow, it proved to be comfortable.

Ceela had not been inside my hut before, and what she saw while we worked on the saddle she didn't like. With the first heavy wind, she told me with words and mimicry, the entire roof would come loose and fly away. Also, in a rainstorm it would leak. Both things would happen unless I tied the palm leaves together in a certain way, which she showed me how to do.

The hut's greatest fault, however, was its lack of paint, inside and out. We talked about this problem for weeks, whenever she came to ride the stallion, which was almost every day.

She wished that I would paint the threshold, the beams that supported the lintel, and the lintel itself a bright sea blue. I had no objection until she explained that blue was the favorite color of the goddess Ix Chel.

"The one in the clearing?" I asked, trying hard to disguise my feelings. "Ix . . . Ix . . . whatever her name?"

"Ix Chel," Ceela said eagerly. "Blue is her magical color. It brings life and much happiness."

Remembering the hideous stone image in the jungle, the eyes that held me with their evil glance, the snakes that coiled about the loathsome body, I felt like tearing at my hair.

"Ix Chel brings many children to people," she said.

"I am the one who is living in this hut," I answered. "It is my house."

Ceela fell silent. She started to say something and stopped. There were tears in her eyes when she turned away from me.

Could she think, I asked myself, that one day she would live in the hut as my wife? Was this why she had given me so many presents, done so much for me?

Not knowing what to say, I took her hand in mine. It was very small and cold. But she pulled away, and the next moment she ran off through the meadow, crossed the stream, and was gone.

After three days, during which Ceela didn't come into my hut, the language lessons continued, and I soon built up a good vocabulary. It became possible for me to put sentences together, copying the nouns and verbs that I heard her use. Just as important, I began to think in Maya, not in Spanish, and in this time, thinking thus, learned something about the island and much about Ceela Yaxche.

She lived more than a league away, with her grandfather, who was sick, her grandmother, and two unwed aunts, who were old, very old. When she was ten, in the middle of the night the top of the volcano had blown away, scattering fire in all directions. The fire and the dust and flowing rock had engulfed their *milpa* and left her mother and father and two brothers dead.

The fire and dust killed many others. The ones who weren't killed fled to the nearby village of Ixpan and beyond, all except what remained of her family. The grandfather, a stubborn and fearless man, built a temporary shelter as near as he could to the old one and remained there with Ceela's grandmother and two aunts, though the volcano smoked day and night, planning that someday he would return to his ruined home.

I learned that we lived on the Island of the Seven Serpents, which accounted for the seven serpents that writhed about the stone goddess Ix Chel. It was about twenty leagues from south to north, eight leagues from west to east, and at the far northern end stood a habitation of many temples and many people called the City of the Seven Serpents, the place I had seen on my return from the volcano.

I also learned something that disturbed me greatly. The natives of this vast temple city were unfriendly, especially toward those who lived on the mainland to the west. Not only unfriendly; they went on regular raids to the mainland and returned with hordes of slaves, whom they sacrificed on their many altars, cutting out their hearts with stone knives.

When I discovered this, the task I had set for myself seemed far beyond my powers or that of a saint or of a dozen saints.

I learned that Ceela and her two aunts supported the family. The aunts wove dresses that Ceela took to the market in Ixpan along with wild honey she gathered in the jungle and put in gourds she had painted herself. The hours left over from these duties she spent with Bravo and me.

Ceela was not an untutored girl, as at first I had thought. Her grandfather had been a priest, before he became old and sick, with the responsibility for the village festivals connected with planting and harvesting, for all the gods who watched over the fields, such as Chac, the god of rain; Hobnil, the patron god of beekeepers; Yum Kaax, god of corn; Xipe Totec, the terrible god of spring, whose effigy had to be clothed in

153

the skins of sacrificial victims. Also the Thirteen Gods of the Upper World, the Nine Gods of the Lower World, and numerous others.

The grandfather had passed on some of his knowledge to Ceela, so she knew the gods by name and spoke of them often. Of them all, however, she worshiped Ix Chel, goddess of childbearing and the moon, whose magical color was blue. She wanted to paint the doorway Ix Chel's favorite color and I invited her to do so — to paint the whole hut blue, if she wished, though it was not to my liking.

One morning while I was grooming Valiente's silky coat, she appeared with three brushes, one of them made of bristles taken from a peccary, two brushes of palm thatch, and gourds filled with rock ground up into a powder. She mixed blue powder with water and daubed the outside walls and the doorway, threshold, and lintel; daubed them twice over.

Then she did something that astounded me. She painted the inside walls a shining white, and astounded me more by painting upon them pictures of Bravo grazing in the meadow, Bravo running with his tail and mane flying in the wind. And, biggest of all, Ceela herself on the stallion's back, riding under a blue sky among blue trees.

She painted with many colors. There were splashes of green and yellow and red, red even in the stallion's mane, and red glints in his eyes. On the deerskin saddle she painted the black spots of a jaguar. Her dress was green dotted with yellow, and in her hair were yellow flowers. The hut reeled and danced with color. It was all fanciful, but still Bravo looked like a stallion and Ceela looked like a girl.

I asked her who had taught her to paint.

"My aunt taught me when I was six. She gave me a brush and paint on the feast day of the god of art. I looked at her. She said, 'Don't stare at me. Take the brush and dip it in the color and paint.'

" 'Where?' I asked.

" 'Anywhere,' she replied.

"So I did. I painted on the wall right beside her."

"What?"

"A dog. It was lying in the doorway asleep. It was an old dog and ugly and had only one ear, since once it was in a fight with a jungle cat. But I painted so it had two ears and was not so ugly and was young again."

"Why," I asked, "when the dog was really old and ugly and had only one ear, why did you paint it to look different?"

"Because when it died then I would remember it as a pretty dog and it would go into the sky young and with two ears."

"To the Thirteen Gods in the sky?"

Ceela nodded. "But my grandfather made me paint it over," she said. "He didn't mind if I painted the gourds to sell the honey in, but he thought for a girl to paint figures on a wall was wrong."

"Your pictures make these walls look fine," I said. "Perhaps you'll paint a picture of our friend Valiente, with his long tail and very long snout which he can move around like a finger."

"When?"

"Now. Any time," I said, and recalling my remark about the hut being mine, "When you come to see me I hope you'll think of this place as yours, too."

She tossed her hair back from her face. "I do not come here to see you as much as to see the horse."

Deep in her honest eyes was a flash of fire.

"When you come to see the horse," I said, "the hut is yours."

The time had come, I decided, for me to use the language I had taken the trouble to learn for the purpose I had learned it, which was to explain to Ceela the meaning of Christ's life and teachings.

Accordingly, the next afternoon, before she had a chance to ride Bravo, I took her to the headland. On the way I caught several flies, of which there were many, and clapped them into a gourd half-filled with water.

Together we climbed to the rock where the cross stood. It had rained that morning, and the air was fresh with the smell of the sea. Gulls circled overhead and sandpipers ran along the beach, but there were no sounds even from the waves.

I waited until Ceela grew tired of the game she had started to play with a handful of blue pebbles. I then explained to her how Christ had died on the cross, like the one that stood before us.

The medal that showed the figure of Our Lord on the cross, the only thing I had saved the morning of the wreck, I took off and put in her hand and told her as I had done before that the medal she held was an image of Christ on the cross.

Then I said that when Christ died, at that moment, at midday with the sun shining, the sky grew dark and the earth shook and the hill where the cross stood was rent asunder.

Ceela clasped her hands together.

"They buried Christ," I said, "in a tomb hewn out of the rock, and in front of it they rolled a large stone. Then, on the third day, while the sun rose, watchers saw that the stone had been rolled back and the tomb was empty, that Christ had risen from the dead."

Her eyes grew wide as I said the last words, but she was puzzled, as I knew she would be. I let all the flies out of the gourd save one. The one that was left I held under the water until its wings went limp. Then I put the fly in the palm of my hand. I had seen Las Casas perform this little act before a class of children in the city of Seville.

"It looks dead," I told Ceela. "But it is not dead."

My hand and the last of the sun's rays warmed the fly. It moved its wings and legs, rubbed its eyes, then suddenly rose and flew away.

Ceela laughed, happy that it had gone. But as far as I could tell, she made no connection between what had happened and the resurrection of Christ.

"We have a god who went off, too," she said. "Only he didn't fly. He built a large raft of snakeskin and sailed away." She pointed toward the east. "He sailed in that direction on his snakeskin raft. But some day he will come back, everyone says. I hope that this is true. His name is Kukulcán. He is the Feathered Serpent."

Kukulcán! Another name to add to the list of Maya gods, to the dozens, to the hundreds of gods, one for each minute of the day, who controlled everything the

Maya did from the time they awakened in the morning until they went to sleep at night and then while they slept. How possibly could one God take the place of a multitude of gods?

"The man," she said, "who flew away like a fly. What did he do before that time? Was he . . ."

I interrupted her. "He didn't fly away like a fly."

"Was he a high priest, an *ahkin*?"

"No, He was a humble man who worked with His hands and went around talking to people all over the countryside."

She looked at the medal I had given her. "Our high priests are lords and they do not walk around talking to people in the countryside or anywhere else. They live in big temples and stay there and talk to the gods. Only to the gods."

"Christ talked to anyone who would listen to Him," I said. "Do you wish to know what He talked about?"

She nodded.

"Christ went out in the hills," I said, "and prayed all night. Then He came back and talked to people."

Ceela picked up the blue stones she had set aside and began to play with them.

"Christ told those who listened, 'Love your enemies, do good to those who hate you, bless those who curse you, give to everyone who begs from you. And from him who takes away your cloak, do not withhold your coat as well. And as you wish that men would do to you, do so to them.' "

Ceela smiled, showing her white teeth, and looked up at me. I saw that she had understood little of what I had said. And why should she understand? The words were there, proper enough, but their meaning was lost. I would need to recast each sentence and explain it as I went along.

"We Maya have many gods," she said, tossing the blue stones into the sea. "And you have only one."

She sounded as if she felt sorry for me.

I had lost my rosary in the wreck of the *Santa Margarita,* so now that I was in possession of a small stone hammer and a supply of stingray spines, I set about the making of one, using stones from the beach for the beads. For the paternoster, the largest bead on the string, I used a piece of driftwood that may have come from the caravel.

It was while I was finishing the rosary that Ceela appeared. I hadn't seen her for two days, since the afternoon on the headland, and I had begun to think that she might be angry because of something I had said. Such was not the case.

She came into the meadow, swinging her arms and singing some odd, strange song. On her head, balanced as neatly as if it were tied there, was a large bundle. I got up and went to meet her and offered to carry the burden, which seemed to be heavy. She refused my help, saying that Mayan men did not carry bundles.

These words should have warned me of what was to come.

In the bundle were a breechclout, a sheaf of gaudy feathers, two painted blue ear plugs, and two anklets made of blue stone. The *mastil,* a band five fingers wide and long enough to be wound about the waist three times and passed between the legs, was also blue—the favorite color, I remembered, of the goddess Ix Chel.

Ceela, greatly pleased with her handiwork, waited for me to be pleased, so I spent some time thinking up compliments. Then I put on the anklets, stepped inside the hut, and got myself into the breechclout, which wasn't as easy as it may sound, and came back to be admired.

When this was attended to, Ceela said, "Now we must make holes in your ears for the plugs, which come from the bones of the jaguar." She drew forth a stone knife, tipped with obsidian.

I was silent.

"The holes do not hurt much," Ceela promised, feeling that I was in need of assurance. "And it takes little time. In five days the holes will be ready. Then I will put the plugs into your ears."

"We will make the holes for my birthday," I said.

"When will that be?"

"Next year," I said.

"I will remember," Ceela informed me. "Now, tomorrow I will make a cloak, and when you wear it with your anklets and ear plugs and the *mastil,* you will look like a Maya. It can be white or black, this cloak. Black is for a warrior. But you are not a warrior. Blue is the best color for you. A blue cloak!"

"White," I said, again remembering Ix Chel. "And please make it a big cloak."

"Yes," she said, "for you are very big, twice as big as the Maya." She was silent for a moment, and then, fearing that I would think poorly of them, quickly added, "But they are strong, the Maya. They can run all day and all the night, and for a week they go without water, even a mouthful."

162

I had the impression, as she stood solidly upon the earth before me, broad of shoulder and the strong color of bronze in the sunlight, that she herself could accomplish all these things.

She had brought powdered yellow rock and a gourd filled with sooty scrapings, which she mixed together into a thin brown paste. While she went on about the Mayan men, she began a picture of Valiente. He was asleep in one corner of the hut, with his long tail looped over his head, but she painted him from memory as she had seen him once at dusk fishing in the stream, crouching on the bank, ready to pounce upon his prey.

He was a muddy brown with a black tail, when she had finished, and looked more like a jaguar than a member of the raccoon family, yet he brightened up the wall with his shining eyes and ferocious teeth and black-banded tail, which looked twice as long as the one he owned.

In return for all the things she had given me, I took off the rosary I had just finished and hung it around her neck. I said nothing to her about its meaning and the way it was to be used, deciding that this could wait for a better time. She was pleased with it.

The next morning, while opening a mess of oysters I had gathered in the mangroves, I happened upon a pearl, the shape of a filbert nut and amber in color. I drilled a hole, and when Ceela came the next day I took the wooden paternoster bead from her rosary and in its place fastened the large amber pearl.

She took the rosary and, smiling, ran the beads through her fingers, happy with what she thought was only a pretty necklace, prettier now by far with its shining pearl. I placed it around her neck and then kissed her upon the forehead, at which she stepped back and gave me a strange look.

I still said nothing about the beads and how she was to use them, planning to do so after I had talked to her again. Perhaps on the headland, when we knelt before the cross.

Soon after she had gone I experienced a sudden and severe shock. I had lifted up my sleeping mat and was about to take it outdoors to air in the sun when I noticed that the earth beneath it had been disturbed. Upon looking closer, I found half-buried there, where I lay my head at night, a small wooden image of Ix Chel, much like the image in the jungle.

With great distaste I dug it up, walked down to the beach, and threw it far out into the sea. But the image did not sink. As I turned away, it was bobbing about from wave to wave, moving toward shore.

A worse shock lay in store for me.

The next morning Ceela came singing through the meadow with green shoots for the stallion and stood at the door of my hut, smiling. I first was aware of the enveloping odor of burning copal. Then, as she fondled the beads around her neck, I noticed that strung beside the amber pearl, the paternoster, was a small wooden figure, an image of the goddess Ix Chel.

Though sorely tempted to berate her, to snatch the hateful image from her neck, I did neither. I stood and smiled back at her and thought that, with the dew in her hair and the early sun shining on her gold-bronze skin, she was a beautiful girl. And very, very young. It was meet that I should exercise some measure of the Christian charity that I was so wont to preach.

That night, however, I could not sleep. I saw the goddess, festooned with the seven writhing snakes, as she stood with her evil gaze fixed upon me. I saw her hanging from the rosary, blasphemously beside the paternoster, about Ceela's young neck.

At dawn, I arose with the resolve to destroy the stone image of the goddess Ix Chel.

I'd had no previous dealings with powder other than watching fireworks set off on feast days and the blasting done on Isla del Oro, so I removed with great care the top from one of my powder kegs and carefully fitted it with two fuses, two because I feared that one might fail me. I put the lid back and sealed it tight with sea mud.

Long before I reached the jungle I smelled the odor of burning copal. It came from a bowl at the feet of Ix Chel. I did not look at the goddess. I put the keg on the ground beside the fire I had brought in the conch shell I once had used at the volcano. I walked around the image, seeking a place to use it.

Behind the clawed feet of the goddess, between them and a nest of sleeping lizards made of stone, was a small space. Into it I set the powder keg. I made sure that the fuses were properly fixed, as I had seen Guzmán fix them at the mine, so that they would burn in an unbroken course.

I then stood off and surveyed everything that lay around me, making sure that there was no obstacle to stumble over, that I was certain which way to flee once the fuses were set.

The sun shone on the red and blue image that towered above me in all of its terror and dreadful meaning—the seven writhing serpents, the many-winged monster, the bloody claws.

I took up the coals, only to find, to my dismay, that they had died away while I stood there. Fortunately, the copal still burned, and with it I lighted each fuse, waited until the powder hissed, then turned and ran.

I chose the tangled path that led toward the beach. I came to a ceiba tree, whence I had a good view of the image, and dodged behind it. The fuses sputtered, faded away, sputtered once more, giving off a shower of bright sparks. The reek of powder took the place of sweet-smelling copal.

I waited. Moments passed. Cautiously, I took one step from behind the ceiba tree onto the trail, from where I gained a full view of the image and the rock that held the gunpowder.

I had taken a second cautious step when a burst of brilliance engulfed the image and the jungle around. A rush of air swept past me, tearing at my clothes, and at once the earth beneath my feet shook with a mighty roar that sent me reeling. Gray smoke shut out the sky. Pieces of stone came down like rain. The roar ended and returned as wandering echoes.

There was little left of the image—a sifting of blue dust, one claw, one serpent's head. An eye, which no longer would have the power to hold me, I picked out from the pile of dust and threw far away into the brush.

The jungle was quiet for a while. Then a bird sang and the macaws went on with their morning chatter. The gray smoke drifted off among the trees. As I stood looking at the pile of rubble, I felt that I had done a worthy deed, yet some of my anger had left me. In its place came a nagging sense of failure. I had destroyed the stone image, but not the longings that would still lie deep in the heart of the girl who worshiped her. These I had not touched.

I took the trail to the headland and stood before the cross. I stood there and thought of Moses. How he came down from the mountain with tablets written by the hand of God, only to find that his people were worshiping a golden calf. That he thereupon broke the tablets and burned the image with fire and ground it to powder. Yes, it was true what Moses had done in his wrath. But I was not Moses, and Ceela was an Indian girl and not the people of Israel. Suddenly, I felt self-righteous.

I got down on my knees and prayed, asking God for mercy and guidance. When I got back to my hut, Ceela was waiting for me. She looked frightened.

"I thought that it was the volcano," she said. "But my grandfather pointed and told me, see, the smoke rises straight up from the volcano and no fire runs down its sides like the time when it was bad."

There was no way to explain gunpowder to her, and I was now too ashamed to tell her all that I had done.

"What did your grandfather think it was?" I asked her.

"He thinks that it was a noise that one of the gods made. Perhaps Itzamná, the great Lord and God."

There were many on the island who thought the same, that mighty Itzamná, Emperor of the Universe, exalted God of the Thirteen Gods of the Upper World and the Nine Gods of the Lower World, that Itzamná had wrathfully caused the thunder. There was, however, one who did not. His name was Guillermo Cantú, a native of Spain.

Cantú appeared the next day at noon, while I was fishing along the estuary. A large red canoe with six men swinging paddles swiftly rounded the northern arm of our little cove and floated to rest not twenty paces from where I stood.

Cantú sat in the prow, chin resting on his knees, and for a moment I took him to be a part of the canoe, its figurehead. Then two of the paddlers slid into the water, lifted him to their shoulders, and set him gently on the shore.

So suddenly did all this take place that I had no chance to be frightened, no time to drop the fishing line, to gather myself together and disappear into the jungle. There magically in front of me were six men painted black and a dwarf who barely reached my belt. A lump with two legs and two long arms, yet surprisingly graceful as he came toward me.

He spoke first, in a high dwarflike voice. His words

came tumbling out, not in Maya as I had expected, but in a language that I did not understand. Through fear and ignorance, I remained silent while the dwarf gave me a puzzled look. His eyes were almond-shaped, a luminous brown, large, beautiful, unexpected in a dwarf, and too beautiful for a man.

He tried again. It was a different language he spoke this time, and, though I still failed to understand it, thinking it might be German, there was a lilting tone to his voice that sounded familiar.

I said to him in my native tongue, "I am a Spaniard. My name is Julián Escobar. From the city of Seville."

"A Spaniard!" he exclaimed. "Seville. Mother of Our Lord."

Tears showed in the dwarf's eyes and, suddenly overcome by emotion, he glided forward and threw his arms about my waist in a stout *embrazo*.

"I took you for a Rhinelander. Your hair and eyes. A blond Rhinelander."

The dwarf loosened his grip on my waist—he could reach no higher—and stepped back. He bowed, touching his forehead on the sand. "Your servant," he said, "Don Guillermo Cantú. Also a native of Seville. Once a student of law at Salamanca."

He paused to run stubby fingers through his beard, which was black, pointed, and well kept. In one ear he wore a plug of green turquoise edged with gold. His cloak was trimmed with green feathers and made of two small jaguar skins, the tails hanging down behind him.

"But I greet you now," Cantú said, "not as a student but in the exalted role of adviser to those who govern

170

the City of the Seven Serpents, as well as many islands hereabouts and far lands to the west."

He glanced over his shoulder toward the paddlers, four of them seated in the canoe and two standing beside it, all of them listening, but to no avail, since the dwarf was speaking in the choicest of Sevillian accents.

"Govern is perhaps not the word," Cantú went on, "for at present the city is in turmoil. Xpan, who ruled as king for many years, is dead this last month, and we have no king; only a score and more of pretenders who ache to kill each other and, it is to be hoped, will, all at once."

In the meadow the stallion neighed. Soon afterward, Ceela came out of the jungle with a bundle of shoots balanced on her head and stopped to feed him. I waved to her, but whether or not she saw me, she didn't answer.

Having recovered somewhat from the shock I had just suffered, and determined to continue the friendly course our talk was taking, I asked Cantú if he, too, had been the victim of a shipwreck.

"Three years ago next month," he said, turning to point. "There in the channel and in broad daylight. All hands saved by Maya fishermen, twenty-one of us. But saved for a worse fate. Carted off to the City of the Seven Serpents, which lies ten leagues northward, and there sacrificed to the gods. All except Guillermo Cantú, for dwarfs are venerated here among the Maya, unlike Seville, where they're the butt of many a scurrilous joke."

"We are both castaways," I ventured.

"Brother Sevillanos," said the dwarf as he again glided forward and for a moment clasped me stoutly around the waist. "Brother Spaniards!"

I had caught a small flounder while fishing the estuary. It lay on the bank, baking in the bright morning sun. The dwarf walked over and dashed sea water upon it, which stirred the fish to life.

"How long have you been a resident of the island?" he asked.

"Since early in September."

"Strange that I heard nothing until last night. News of you arrived by runner from the village of Ixpan while I was eating dinner. Since I knew that the horrendous commotion was caused neither by the volcano nor by thunder from the skies, I was certain that it was caused by an explosion of gunpowder. And gunpowder, I reasoned, must belong to a Spaniard, since powder is unknown upon the island. But this morning, when I first set eyes upon you—tall and blond and blue-eyed—I doubted my reasoning."

"Little wonder."

"And why did you explode the gunpowder? To attract attention to your plight?"

Not knowing whether or not he, too, had become a devotee of the goddess Ix Chel, I gave him an evasive answer.

"Is there powder left?"

"A keg."

"A little keg or a big keg?"

"A medium-sized keg."

It must have been at this moment that the monstrous

plan took final shape in his mind. He had been watching the six paddlers. He now turned his full gaze upon me. It traveled from my head to my bare feet, inch by inch, slowly, as if he had not seen me before.

Cantú, the dwarf, glanced up at me. I noticed that the candor I had first seen in his eyes had given way to a look of duplicity. He walked around me in a wide circle, scratching his bumpy head, examining me as if I were a statue.

He said, "Centuries ago the lord of this island was Kukulcán, the same lord, incidentally, who is known among the Aztecs as Quetzalcoatl. He was a real man, this Kukulcán, no mythical god. He was a captain, and he came mysteriously from out of the north into the land of the Maya."

"I have heard of him," I said, nodding toward Ceela, who had appeared and stood behind the dwarf, staring at him in awe. "From this girl."

Cantú went on as if I had not spoken. "Kukulcán ruled this island for years. Then, under the influence of strong drink, he committed disgraceful acts. So remorseful was he when at last his sense returned that he made a raft for himself and alone sailed off into the east."

The dwarf looked in that direction and pointed with a stubby finger. He glanced at Ceela.

"You know this girl?"

"For months."

"Does she understand Spanish?"

"Not a word."

"Excelente," said the dwarf. "Kukulcán, the captain and lord, sailed off. But his words of farewell to those who tearfully watched him go—and this is important, so listen to me carefully. His last words were these: 'I leave you now but I shall come again. I will come from the east. You will find me in the body of a young man, younger than I, a tall youth with golden hair whose eyes are blue.' "

Walking back and forth, the dwarf surveyed me once more; minutely, this time, as if he were at the market about to purchase a slave. He did everything except ask me to open my mouth while he examined my teeth.

At last he turned to Ceela and spoke in Maya. "You have heard of Kukulcán?"

"Oh, yes. Since the time I was a child."

"Do many people know about him?"

"Everyone everywhere knows of Kukulcán. Soon, when three suns have come and gone, will be his feast day. Already in the village of Ixpan they have begun the celebration."

"The people pray for Kukulcán's return?"

"Every year we pray."

"They also pray for his return in the City of the Seven Serpents," said the dwarf. "They sing and dance and burn copal before the temples."

"This I have heard, though I have not seen it with my own eyes."

The dwarf plucked me by the sleeve and said in his fine Spanish accent, "You see that Captain Kukulcán is

175

a living legend. Even this country girl knows about him and prays for his return."

It was not what he had said before nor his words now to Ceela that gave me the first hint that something dire was afoot. It was the way he looked at me that brought sweat to my brow.

The dwarf said, "Do you understand? Do you see what goes through my mind?"

"Dimly," I replied.

"But you see it nonetheless," said the dwarf. "It is a bold undertaking. If it fails, we are confronted with disaster. You will die and I will die with you. We will both die on the sacrificial stone, our hearts removed with an obsidian knife."

I looked away from him across the strait to the far mountains veiled in mist. I tried to conceal the emotions that seethed within me. I must have failed, for at once the dwarf's manner changed.

His enormous eyes clouded over. His lips, which were stained purple with some kind of fruit he had eaten, tightened. He was no longer the new-won friend, a brother Sevillano sharing memories of a happy past, a Spaniard offering succor to another Spaniard, but an ambitious and cunning rogue.

"I see that you are confused," he said in his shrill voice, "so may I be of assistance. Your presence on this island is known. If you refuse the role I have devised, the high priests will deal with you. It may be tomorrow or it may be a week from now, but they will surely send warriors to take you away to the City of the Seven Serpents, and there, amid the jubilation of thousands, sacrifice you to the gods, as they did all my companions, twenty-one of them, not so long ago."

The beach was quiet save for the sound of water lapping against the canoes. Ceela stood at a distance from us, in awe of the dwarf, who was now scuffling his feet in the sand, waiting impatiently for me to answer. There was a thundering in my head. I could not open my mouth to say a word.

Cantú, the dwarf, said, "You have doubts. Speak up."

"I am not a Maya," I answered at last.

"So much the better. If you were a Maya, you would then look like one of the six warriors who stand in front of you."

The six were staring at me in awe. They had put down their paddles and were holding long spears tipped with stones and macaw feathers. Their bodies, which were painted black, gleamed in the hot sun.

"Note," said the dwarf, "that each has a prominent nose and a forehead that slants back and comes to something of a point at the crown. They also have crossed eyes. This is the Maya look. Fortunately, it is not your look. You fit the legend precisely. You are young, tall, white, blue-eyed, and golden-haired."

Struck dumb by the man's audacity, I had trouble summoning a second objection to his plan, though a dozen crowded my mind. At last I said, "I do not like the thought of placing myself in the role of a mountebank."

"Would you prefer to have your chest ripped open

and your heart plucked out? Are your scruples that keen?"

"No," I said, and fell silent.

The dwarf prodded me. "What else confuses you?" he asked.

"I am not fit, not suited to be a god. I am not a god."

"It is not what you are that matters. It is what the people think you are."

"The plan is preposterous," I said.

"We shall see." The dwarf drew himself up and puffed his cheeks. "Your choice, *amigo,* is simple. You accept the role I have chosen for you, or you die on the sacrificial stone as a common castaway. As for me, if by chance you wonder, all I need to do is to return to the City of the Seven Serpents with the news that another Spaniard has been cast upon the shore."

He motioned to the warriors, two of whom trotted over and raised him to their shoulders.

"Three days from now in the morning I will be back," he said, "with many warriors, musicians, and three high priests. Be ready. Seat yourself upon the horse, the one I caught a glimpse of a moment ago standing beside your hut. Grease his coat so that it shines. Comport yourself like a god." He paused to give me a threatening look. "If you are not here, we will find you."

The warriors placed him in his canoe and they all took up their paddles, continuing to stare at me as they moved away, as if already they had decided that I *was* the god Kukulcán. The dwarf waved. Ceela and I watched them until they disappeared behind the promontory.

She had understood nothing of the conversation, but she had heard the name Kukulcán spoken a number of times. She asked me if the dwarf's visit had something to do with the god's feast day. I told her that it had. I decided to say no more.

"The dwarf is a big man among the noble rulers of this island," she said. "He is very big; my grandfather has told me."

"I noticed that you stood off and treated him with respect."

"It is wise," she said, "to be respectful when noble people are about."

I looked at her broad, handsome brow and asked her why, since it was the fashion of the Mayans, her mother had not changed its shape.

"She wished to do this," Ceela explained, "but my grandfather would not let her. He said that heads were meant to be as they had been given to us. He said that to change their shape was vain, an insult to the gods."

Ceela pushed back her shock of hair and felt her head and smiled. "Do you like it this way?" she asked.

"Yes, exactly that way," I said. "Tell me, does your grandfather have crossed eyes and a head that slants?"

She nodded. "Yes, he has one like that because it was done to him when he was a baby. His mother did this with the boards, and she likewise hung a pebble in front of his eyes and encouraged him to look at it, so his eyes became crossed."

Bravo came running along the shore, splashing through the waves, and stopped in front of us, dripping sea water.

"I feared when the dwarf came with the warriors," Ceela confessed, "that he had come to take you away." She blushed at these words and quickly added, "What would happen if he came back and took Bravo away?"

That night I never closed my eyes in sleep. It was not that I lay awake trying to decide what I would do. It was clear that I could not stay where I was. Nor could I hope to escape by fleeing into the jungle or taking to sea on a raft. I had no choice except to play out the role the dwarf had devised for me, wildly preposterous though it was. Either that or to give up my life on a sacrificial stone.

Three days later, in midmorning, as instructed by
Cantú, I was on the beach when his flotilla of red canoes rounded the promontory.

I sat astride the stallion, whose coat I had brushed till
it shone, whose mane Ceela had braided and woven
with ribbons of blue cloth. His tail was combed and his
hooves polished. He looked magnificent, a Pegasus, the
perfect mount for a god.

As for myself I was dressed in my makeshift boots,
the blue cloak Ceela had sewn for me, which was far too
small, and the frayed breechclout. I didn't look at all as
a god should look—imperious, defiant, fashioned of ice
and fire. Nor, alas, did I feel like one.

The flotilla sped shoreward, one canoefollowing hard
upon the other. I counted ten, twenty, thirty-three. With
feathered pennons flying from prow and stern, laden
with warriors painted black and musicians painted
green, to the swish of broad-bladed paddles, the rattle
of shakers and the beat of drums, of conch-shell horns
bellowing, they came toward us as if they were charging
an enemy and we ourselves were that enemy. To make
this seem even more like the beginning of a battle, the
canoes, moving as one, pulled up when they neared the

shore, and the phalanx of warriors, no longer smiting the air and the sea, laid down their paddles and grasped long spears, which they brandished, meanwhile sending forth blood-chilling cries.

Ceela, who stood beside the stallion, one hand clutching his mane, retreated and took up a place behind me. For moments I myself was seized with an impulse to retreat, to turn and flee into the jungle, even though I were pursued by a hundred warriors. It was possible that the dwarf's plan had failed at the very beginning, that the flotilla had come to take me prisoner.

My apprehension was soon dispelled. While Ceela watched with open fear and I hid mine as best I could, two Indians, as they had done on our first meeting, gathered up Cantú, the dwarf, and set him down upon the beach. I recognized him only by his shape. He carried a feathered cane and wore a feathered headdress much larger than he was, adorned with the hooked beak of a macaw. Through this mask he now addressed me, his words sounding more birdlike than human.

"Captain Kukulcán," he said, speaking in Spanish, "you make a godly impression as you sit there in the sun on your black Arabian steed. Two of the three priests who are assembled in the canoe directly behind me are amazed by what they behold. So amazed, in fact, that they are speechless."

The priests were huddled together in the bow of a red canoe that was carved in the shape of a giant two-headed serpent. They wore elaborate masks covered with gaudy feathers, two of the masks representing jaguars with teeth bared and one the visage of an araguato, a howling monkey.

"Two of the priests," the dwarf continued, "think that you and the horse are one. God-horse, a horse-god, inseparable, one and the same."

Six warriors now gathered around the priests and carried them ashore and set them down with great care, as if they were fragile objects that might fall apart.

"Despite amazement at your godlike appearance," Cantú said, "we have a serious problem. It is the priest Chalco. He's the one in the monkey mask. Without the masks they all look pretty much alike—slanted foreheads, ear plugs, teeth set with turquoise. It took me weeks to tell one from the other. But Chalco you will come to recognize, for he is prone to breathe through his mouth, making a hissing sound as he does so."

The three stood motionless not a dozen paces from where I sat astride my nervous mount. Their hands were concealed; the tails of their enormous headdresses trailed long feathers in the sand. The sun fell full upon them, and through the wide slits in their masks I could see that two were gazing at me in wild astonishment. The third priest, however, the one with the araguato-like visage, stood with his eyes averted, looking off somewhere in the distance.

"This Chalco doubts that you are the god Kukulcán," the dwarf said, his words tumbling out. "Chalco's doubts are based upon a powerful ambition. Maliciously, he aspires to the lordship of the city; in time, in time, to be, God forbid, a god himself. At this moment you are in the way. We are in the way. But events favor us. We can count upon two of the priests, Hexo and Xipan, both of whom would like to see Chalco catch his nose in the door. Furthermore, this is the feast day of Kukulcán. What better time for you on your beautiful black steed to ride forth into the City of the Seven Serpents?"

The priests, all three of them, were watching us through their slitted masks. Perhaps for their astonishment, perhaps because he now sensed victory, the dwarf began to speak in a lively tone, so cheerily that I expected to see him break out into a dance.

"Señor, brother Sevillano," he said, "do exactly as I tell you. It is *absolutamente necesario.* First, display the steed. He is one of the keys that unlock the door to the kingdom. Slowly circle about us. Then gallop off along the beach. Then return and assume a position in front of the priests, perhaps a trifle closer to them than you are at present, for they must clearly hear each word you speak."

I took a firm seat, a good hold upon the reins. Behind me, in the throes of fear and excitement, Ceela said something under her breath that I only half caught. But I did not ask her to repeat it, thinking that it was an unseemly moment for me, a newborn god, to answer questions.

Sitting tall and stiff-backed as I had often seen Don Luis ride, I made a circle, as I had been instructed to do, aware of silent wonderment on the part of two of the priests and the studied indifference of Chalco. I spurred the stallion into a gallop, sped down the beach, and returned, splashing through the waves, to face the three priests and Cantú, the dwarf.

Birdlike, Cantú hopped forward and with bowed head whispered further instructions. They were simple. I followed them at once, using the words he put in my mouth but, to his immense surprise, speaking them in Maya. "I have come back," I said, "after many years in eastern lands. I appear, as you can see and as I promised, in a different body, the body of a young man blue-eyed and white of skin. I come to rule this kingdom once again. My name is Kukulcán."

As I spoke the words "My name is Kukulcán," there came from behind me a moan of surprise and alarm. It was followed almost at once by a piercing cry. Turning in the saddle, I saw that Ceela lay stretched upon the sand. I jumped from the stallion's back, forgetting that I was now a god, and stooped to take her up. But with a fearful look she was on her feet, running away along the shore, then through the meadow. At the edge of the jungle she paused to glance back. I waved to her, but she raised her hands to her eyes, as if to shut me out, then disappeared among the trees.

The dwarf, in great distress at this interruption, was hopping about with his feathers dragging, so I quickly took up the reins and a godlike pose, which to my surprise came easier to me than it had at first, only moments before.

The words that had shocked Ceela had another and instant effect. As the drums and shakers, which had kept up a steady beat throughout the encounter, fell silent, the three priests turned their backs upon me. Two of them at once; the third grudgingly.

Also about to turn away, but observing my perplexity at the strange behavior of the priests, the dwarf paused. "Henceforth," he said, "no one will look at you face to face. And I will do so only when we're alone, speaking as two Spaniards. It is the custom here in this strange land. *La costumbre.*"

Before turning his back, the dwarf asked my pardon and said, "You speak Maya well. *Perfectamente.* Although Chalco conspires against us, as is to be expected, this has strengthened our hold upon the other two, Hexo and Xipan."

The tide was rising, and with it there suddenly appeared a shoal of bright-colored crabs. Deposited at our feet, they took fright and scuttled off down the beach, save one, larger than my hand, which took up a position nearby. It reared up and fixed its eyes, which sat like jewels at the ends of long stalks, upon me, at the same time challenging my presence with scimitarlike claws.

The dwarf scuttled crabwise across the sand and placed a foot upon the silvery shell, saying, "That much for our friend, whose name I will not mention, for he is listening—the one who breathes through his mouth and makes hissing sounds as he does so."

He then signaled with his feathered cane. Three canoes promptly slid into the beach. They were held together bow and stern by thongs and by a rough-hewn platform of poles built amidships, upon which with some difficulty I urged the stallion. The keg of gun-

187

powder was carried through the waves and carefully stowed in a fourth canoe.

The conch-shell horns sounded; shakers and drums took up their beat.

From my precarious perch beside Bravo, I watched my home disappear. First the headland and the wooden cross; then my doorless hut, through which Valiente had come and gone at his pleasure, on whose walls Ceela had daubed her girlish paintings; then the stream in the meadow and the trail that led to the green jungle, whence she had come bringing gifts. I looked for her in the leafy opening, where I saw or thought I saw a movement among the undergrowth, but it must have been the morning breeze springing up, for she was nowhere to be seen. It was a sad, sad moment for me.

The dwarf, sweating beneath his feathers, said, "We have come this far. Holy Mary, be good to us the rest of the way."

We moved rapidly northward, hugging the coast, through water the color of turquoise, past white caves and stretches of jungle, then clearings where there were clusters of thatched huts, much like the hut I had left, and small farms green with growing crops. People ran to the shore to stare at us. We came to a reef that curved beneath us like a giant fishhook, marked by poles driven into the sea and decorated with tufts of bright feathers.

As we rounded a westward bend in the coast, I saw what seemed to be a cloud lying low above the sea. It was gray in color and oddly shaped, unlike any cloud I had ever seen before. At the same moment, there came to me on the morning breeze a familiar smell.

The dwarf, who stood at my side, his back turned, said, "The odor is copal. And the cloud that you see is not a cloud but the Temple of Kukulcán thrusting upward through the smoke from a thousand burning vessels. Do you recognize it from your previous life? No? Well, you should, for it is said that it has not changed in many centuries, not since your departure from these shores."

The dwarf glanced over his shoulder. Through the slits his eyes squinted up at me with the sly confidence of a man who holds a winning card that he has not yet played.

He said, "I repeat, Señor Capitán, that we two are brothers. Together we rule this kingdom or together we perish. We have convinced two of the priests of your godhead. Now we must convince the populace. In this, the stallion will be of great importance. Therefore, be prepared to mount as we reach the next promontory and come within the sight of those who throng the shore."

He left the platform, crawled forward to where six warriors were wielding paddles, and said something to them. Evidently he asked them to change their pace, for at once we slowed down. The long line of canoes followed slowly in our wake, drums and shakers causing a hellish din.

The canoe behind us drew abreast momentarily and Cantú beckoned for the keg. Then the dwarf returned and set to work with the gunpowder.

"It will awaken the dead," he told me, "and astound the living. I plan to set it off the moment before you ride ashore. It may kill a dozen or so, but this will make it all the more astounding."

He must have seen the expression on my face, for he quickly explained. "The Maya don't look upon death as we Spaniards do. They have much of it. To them, it is a friend. And blood that flows, especially when it flows copiously, fascinates them. You will see much of it before the day is over."

"About the explosion . . ." I said.

"You need not concern yourself with it," the dwarf broke in. "It will take place out of your sight."

"If there's such an explosion, I will not go ashore."

The dwarf turned and, seeing that I meant my words, assured me that he would exercise great care. "No one will be killed; no more than a stray dog," he said.

Watching him as he went on fussing with a contraption that was similar to the one I had made, I wondered what strange dream, what towering ambition, had prompted him to risk his life on the nightmare he was now engaged in.

I was emboldened to say, flattering him with a title, "You take grave chances, Don Guillermo. Why?"

He answered me promptly. "*Dinero,* señor. Money. Excelentes, castellanos, cruzados, doubloons, ducats, maravedis. Money in all its marvelous values and forms."

"There are no excelentes or ducats or castellanos on this island," I said. "I know this from my friend, Ceela Yaxche. The natives use cacao beans for money."

"True, Señor Capitán. But cacao can be bartered for precious stones. Emeralds from Tikal. From beyond Tikal come pearls. And there is much gold in lands farther to the south. To the west, the Aztecs have silver in vast quantities. I will trade for these things. Pardon me, señor. We, you and I, will trade for these things. In time we will gather a storeroom stacked with fat chests filled with treasure."

"You risk your life for this?"

"Trout from the stream," the dwarf replied, "cannot be taken in dry breeches."

191

He went on with his preparations, pouring a handful of powder into a fuse, which he then sealed with bees-wax. He said, "You will soon find the position of lord and god tiresome. You will become weary of cross-eyed savages swarming about you. What happens at this time, Capitán? What do you do? Flee with empty arms?"

"I have not planned that far ahead. But offhand, the idea of filling a storehouse with treasure taken from this country does not appeal to me. Indeed, it seems loathsome."

The dwarf gave out one of his small, thin chuckles. "I share with the Emperor Tiberius the thought that the part of a good shepherd is to shear his flock, not to fleece them. Señor Capitán, you and I will be good Tiberian shepherds."

"How many can we shear?" I joked with him.

"Twenty thousand."

"On the island?"

"Thirty thousand."

"All pagans?"

"All."

"Who have never heard of Christ?"

"Not one."

"You have made no effort to spread our Catholic faith?"

"None. Do you think my bowels are made of brass? But there are more pressing issues. One is Moctezuma the Second, Emperor of the Aztecs. His hordes have overrun the mainland. Most of its cities pay him yearly tribute in goods and gold. And his hunger for slaves is insatiable. In the last year, our road weasels report, he sacrificed in one day twenty thousand slaves. Three months ago he sent an army down here to collect slaves from us. But his army was not used to fighting on the sea, so we drowned most of them and took the rest prisoners."

"This emperor who has twenty thousand hearts removed in a single day," I said, thinking for the first time as one who was responsible for the lives of others, "where does he rule?"

"In Mexico—Tenochtitlan, a sky city, situated in the mountains at a height of more than two leagues, some four hundred leagues to the northwest."

"Then he's not a neighbor."

"No, but he has sharp eyes which are fixed upon us, the only city he has not conquered. His army will be back one of these days."

"Who leads this army? Moctezuma?"

"Of course not. He has a palace of fifty rooms, all stuffed with gold. He has an aviary with ten thousand birds. A zoo twenty times the size of ours. Fountains, streams, floating gardens, lakes. And three hundred and fifteen wives. Why would he lead an army and risk his royal neck?"

Our flotilla continued northward at a steady pace to the sound of music and dipping paddles. On our way we passed a stone marker, carved with colored glyphs, which, the dwarf informed me, had been erected to celebrate the victory over Moctezuma's hordes.

"Prisoners from that triumph will be sacrificed today," Cantú said.

He scrambled forward to the bow of the canoe, spoke something to one of the warriors, and scrambled back. He sidled up, stole a quick glance at my skimpy attire.

"Tomorrow, *hombre*, I will see that you are properly clothed. Feathered headdresses by the score, jaguar-skin cloaks, snakeskin sandals, amber bracelets, necklaces of the most precious stones. You may also wish to have your nose pierced for turquoise plugs and your teeth filed and set with jade."

I made no reply to this last suggestion, feeling that it did not require an answer.

"But we have a more serious problem," the dwarf said. "Our Council of Lords is concerned with a coming war with the city of Tikan. The *nacom* in charge of the army sent out three road weasels early last week. These spies returned to report that Tikan is preparing for battle. They are collecting a large store of hornets' nests."

The dwarf paused to flick away a pink insect that was bent on getting into his ear.

"Were you ever bitten by a hornet?" he asked. "Yes? Then you are acquainted with the fiery sting. A hornet's nest is a deadly weapon. Tikan has collected over a hundred. Furthermore, their army is led by one of our countrymen, a Don Luis de Arroyo."

I was not surprised to hear the name spoken. There was, I had always thought, a good chance that Don Luis had somehow survived. My last memory of him on the morning of the shipwreck was the moment when he pushed aside the barber's hand to save himself. He was a man of great determination. Once ashore, he could have managed to make his way into the confidence of the Indians and talk them into an adventurous war.

Calmly I said, "I know Don Luis de Arroyo. We sailed together from Seville. He owned the caravel that sank, the *Santa Margarita.*"

"You know him well, then. Tell me, is he brave? Can he lead Indians into battle?"

"He is a fearless man. And ruthless."

"Xpan's death left us unprepared and without a leader. The Council of Lords would prefer to fight later, when the harvest is over, when our weaponry is in better shape, and the stars are in conjunction. Do you have influence with Arroyo? Could you persuade him to delay his attack?"

"No," I said. "If he knew I was here and in a position of power, it would only encourage him. He would be devious. He would pretend friendship, but only to attack us when we least expect it."

A harsh judgment, but Don Luis de Arroyo had earned it.

"You favor an attack, then? As soon as the stars are favorable?"

"I would not wait on the stars."

I was astounded at myself in urging war upon Don Luis. Astounded that suddenly I had spoken, not as Julián Escobar, a seminarian, a lover of peace, a follower of meek St. Francis, but as the powerful god Kukulcán.

The dwarf thought for a while. "You had cannon aboard the *Santa Margarita*?"

"Many. Three bombards, five brass falconets, others."

"How deep does the *Santa Margarita* lie?"

"At low tide, fifteen feet."

"We have pearl divers here on the island who can dive that deep and stay under water for as long as four minutes at a time. Long enough to fasten ropes around the cannon so that they can be dragged up. With our keg of gunpowder, we will be more than a match for their hundred hornets' nests."

The dwarf, though he was standing near the edge of the platform, gave one of his little jigs, laughed, then fell sober again.

"We have lesser problems that require your counsel," he said. "For one, there is at present a feud between our three ball teams. You have not seen this game. It is not played in Spain. The players are heavily protected by leather padding, scuffle with each other over a ball as big as a melon. The ball is hard, but bounces. The ob-

196

ject is to put it into stone rings at either side of the court. It is . . ."

"What is the feud about?" I broke in, for I could see that he was devoted to the game and was bent on winding away. "What will I have to do with the feud?"

"Everything, *hombre*. The Jaguars and the Hawks are troublemakers. The Eagles . . ."

Cantú, who favored the Eagles, went on further to describe the game and furnish the names of each of the players, their individual merits, ages, and sizes.

"A fine group of young men," he said, concluding his description of the Eagles. "You will soon be cheering for them, I am sure. And also you will admonish the Jaguars and the Hawks, who have swollen *cabezas,* to speak civilly when spoken to. And quit strutting about the city, frightening people and getting into brawls. This should be one of the first things you do, señor."

A commanding, peremptory tone had come into the man's voice. It was annoying. I suddenly foresaw the day when he would be giving me orders instead of suggestions.

"Guillermo Cantú," I said, "henceforth will you address me not as *señor* or *hombre* or *capitán,* but by my proper name."

He turned and glanced up. There was an insolent glint in his eyes.

"What name is that?"

"The name you so thoughtfully bestowed upon me and insisted that I assume."

"All of it?"

"Yes, Señor Cantú, all of it."

"You are not a god yet."

"Nor are you," I answered.

The dwarf came forth with a false smile, smoothed down the feathers on his headdress.

"The time approaches," he said, "when we shall know who is a god and who is not."

"Hurry the moment," I said, "and in the event that your scheme does succeed, there is something I wish you to do. Send canoes to the place where you found me and bring back the girl, Ceela Yaxche, who lives nearby."

"It is too soon to think of such things," the dwarf objected. "Here we teeter on an abyss, and you think of a girl. She is comely, from what I saw of her, but the city is full of comely girls. I can collect fifty in an hour."

"Bring her," I said.

"What if she is needed in the family? Most girls are."

"She *is* needed. So bring the family. All of them."

The dwarf was unhappy.

"And in the hut," I added, "you will find during the day, not at night, a coatimundi. His name is Valiente."

"We have hundreds of the pests in the jungle and many in the streets."

"Bring him," I said. "Bring Ceela. Bring everybody. And send the canoes today."

Grudgingly, Cantú bowed.

Through an opening almost hidden from seaward, so narrow that I could reach out and touch its walls, we entered a small lagoon guarded on two sides by high walls. At the far end of the lagoon, at a distance of half a league or less, stood the City of the Seven Serpents.

The dazzling sight held my tongue.

The dwarf said, "Three years ago when, as a castaway, I first came upon the city, it rendered me speechless too. Speechless I remain. There is nothing in Spain to match it. Nor in France. I have traveled far. Only in the land of Egypt will you find edifices such as greet us now."

Before me, hacked out of the surrounding jungle, stood a central plaza, and facing it on the left and right, two pyramidlike temples that rose to thrice the height of the tallest trees. Broad steps ascended them on the two sides that I could see, ending at the lofty top in a terrace and an ornate structure that the dwarf informed me was the godhouse.

"With luck, we will stand there soon."

There was a stone landing at the far end of the lagoon, where a fleet of canoes was moored. Beyond, leading to the plaza and the two temples, I saw a wide thoroughfare thronged with people.

"Stupendous," said the dwarf. "The greatest gathering since the feast day of lordly Itzamná. They have come from all parts of the island."

At his command—he still spoke in a commanding tone, only a little less peremptory than formerly—I mounted Bravo.

"I had one of the warriors pour out only a third of the keg to complete the bomb," he said. "The rest of the gunpowder we'll use in the cannon when Don Luis de Arroyo and Moctezuma the Second pay us their visits."

As the unwieldy craft nosed into the *embarcadero*, I made ready to ride ashore.

"When the powder explodes," the dwarf said, "—and fervently pray that it will explode, for much depends on it—at that moment when the earth shakes and smoke rises in a stupefying cloud, ride through and emerge on the far side. I will be there to lead you on your way to the Temple of Kukulcán. It's the taller temple, the one on the left. Built, incidentally, in your honor, some four hundred and forty-two years ago, ten years after you fled the island, or so I am told."

The dwarf preceding me, I rode up a wooden ramp, carved with many figures, to a terrace that was seven-sided and paved with wooden blocks. On all of its seven sides were serpents, each alike, carved from stone, with their heads resting on their coiled bodies, their eyes half-closed and mouths agape.

The terrace was empty except for warriors, who, spears in hand, stood guard beside the serpents. The dwarf motioned for me to halt, scrambled to the middle of the terrace, set down the powder, and covered it with his feathered cloak.

The flotilla was now moored in the lagoon. The three priests were huddled on the landing, seemingly awaiting further word from Cantú. They had taken off their masks and, in their feathered headdresses, no longer looked like jaguars and a howling monkey, but more like giant birds of prey.

Beyond the dwarf, from the broad thoroughfare that led to the plaza and the two temples, came a chorus of wild sounds, the cries and shouts and silences of a multitude, swelling and dying away.

In a moment of silence the dwarf drew back his cloak and touched the fuse with tinder. I sat fifty paces away or more, with a tight hold on the stallion. Among my many real and imagined fears was the fear that he might bolt, for I lacked spurs and bit, to which he was accustomed.

The fuses caught, sputtered, apparently went out, then in an instant caught again. The explosion was not so heavy as the one I had set off under the statue of Ix Chel, but it was loud. The stallion reared and shied away. I managed to hold him more by words than by the halter.

Through the cloud of black smoke that rose over the terrace I urged him on. A pair of clowns with false faces and circular stripes around their bodies suddenly appeared in front of me and were joined by a dozen or more musicians. Led by Cantú, the dwarf, the assemblage then moved forward to the rattle of drums and clownish chatter.

These were the only sounds I heard. The bronze-skinned crowd that lined both sides of the thoroughfare was silent. It was the deep silence of awe and adoration.

We had not gone a furlong before the dwarf whispered from his place at Bravo's flank, "The stallion has won the day. The explosion helped. The populace believes that it was the voice of the horse. And you, despite a certain tightness around the mouth, as if you felt the rusty taste of fear, look very much as a god should look. Hold firm, Lord Kukulcán. Have courage. And as our brave forebears on the heights of Granada shouted into the very teeth of the Moors, 'Santiago!' "

Bringing to mind that ancient scene, following the dwarf's admonitions, I held firm and swallowed my fears. The stallion responded. He must have remembered the fiestas in Seville at which he had carried Don Luis through flower-decked streets. He turned his neck and took mincing, sidewise steps, lifting his hooves as if he were treading on snakes.

I was suddenly aware that the silent crowd was watching me from a distance. But when I came upon the people, all of them, on both sides of the thoroughfare, quickly turned their backs. I saw no face except that of a child, a girl of four or five, who gazed up at me with wondering eyes, as if truly I *were* a god. The only god she had ever seen or would ever see again.

Farther along, a boy ran out in great excitement and fell in front of the stallion. He lay stunned. Ordinarily, I would have jumped down and seen to him, but thinking of my new role as mighty Kukulcán, I rode on.

The silent thousands fell in behind us as we moved along—the painted clowns cavorting out in front, the dwarf hobbling along at my side, the priests following close. We came to the broad plaza outlined by columns that were painted a shining red and carved with scenes of battle. The twin temples I had seen from afar, thrusting into the sky through clouds of copal smoke, now stood before me.

The dwarf said, "The citizens are silent, but don't be misled. They are ready to acclaim you. The words now tremble on their lips. Come, and we shall accomplish the final act."

The clowns had disappeared, and the three priests, joined by a dozen or more retainers, had set off up a long flight of stairs that led from the ground to the terrace at the summit of the Temple of Kukulcán.

"Seventy-seven steps," the dwarf said, leading me through the forest of red columns. "There's a shorter way."

We came to the far side of the pyramidlike temple and I followed him into a shadowy passage, just high enough for me to enter if I crouched low over the stallion's neck. It was musty with the smell of bats that clung to the roof and flapped away at our approach.

The dwarf struck light to a wick in a bowl of tallow

and led me upward, round and round in tight circles. The stone walls dripped water. Stalagmites that projected from the earthen floor made it necessary for us to advance with caution.

We came to a series of narrow alcoves through whose openings the light shone, revealing rows of obsidian slabs carved with figures of owls and frogs, other creatures that I could not distinguish. These places, the dwarf told me, held the bodies of dead kings and high priests.

The air grew stale. The dwarf stopped with an exclamation of anger. *"Nombre de Dios,"* he said. "We have taken a wrong turn." His words sounded down the passageway and by some trick came weirdly back to us in decreasing echoes from far above. "We must return. We need to reach the godhouse before the priests."

It was not easy to square the stallion around in the narrow place, with the dwarf shouting instructions. Finally he ran back, holding the light aloft, and I followed. We traveled for half a furlong, to the last of the crypts. There, he took a left turn and, scuttling ahead, urged me on.

With visions of being trapped in miles of tomblike tunnels, I quickly caught up with him and kept hard on his heels. The widening walls no longer dripped water. We came to a large room, where the dwarf's light shone on shelves that rose from floor to ceiling and ran far back into darkness. Upon these racks, their cheekbones touching, were human skulls in endless rows.

"Is this a cemetery?" I asked the dwarf.

"In a way of speaking. The heads, but not the bodies, are brought here when the ceremonies are over."

We reached a wide, heavily carved door. Shoving it open, he said, "Ride! Come to a halt upon the parapet."

Light flooded in through the doorway although the day was sunless. For a moment I was blinded. The stallion neighed and backed off into the darkness. I put hard heels to him. He took only a step toward the door, and there set his hooves. The dwarf shouted, to no avail. Dismounting, I tried to lead him to the doorway, but again he flinched and backed away.

"Time is short," the dwarf shouted. "Tether him here in the alcove. No matter. You cannot appear always on your horse. You cannot take him to bed with you."

I tethered Bravo at the door and stepped out upon the wide stone parapet. Far away to the margin of the sea, to the very reaches of the eye, shimmering red and blue and yellow and turquoise green—all the colors Ceela had painted upon the walls of my hut—lay the walled City of the Seven Serpents.

Below, far down, seeming as small as insects, stood the multitude, a river of insects flowing away in the distance.

The dwarf was at my side. "Raise your hand," he said. "Raise it high."

I had no sooner done so than a chant, like the sound of a distant storm, floated up to me. The chant grew louder, became a shout, then it was a single thunderous word repeated over and over: "Kukulcán! Kukulcán!"

The dwarf cocked his head at the sound. He did his

little jig. "Hexo, Xipan, and Chalco will conduct a vote," he said. "They will confer with the city elders, the *nacom*. The outcome, however, is no longer in doubt."

The priests, toiling up the long steep flight of steps, had nearly reached the terrace upon which we stood. They paused to watch the chanting multitude, all save Chalco, who, dragging his feet, continued slowly on his way.

The three priests in their towering headdresses came together on the terrace. Without a word they bowed to me, to the teeming crowd below, to each other, and turned their backs. They looked insignificant against the vast dome of the sky. Chanting went on, died away, rose up again stronger than before.

"These ceremonies," the dwarf said, "often get out of hand. Also, you will not like what you see. But remember that you are now a god and that gods flourish upon blood."

Off to my right, in front of the godhouse where I stood, at the edge of the terrace in order that the throng could see, was a large, curiously shaped object. I took it to be a decoration or a statue of some Maya god.

"The sacrificial altar," the dwarf said.

It was longer than a man's body, some three feet in width and the same in height, curved upward in the center.

Seven priests came through a doorway at the far end of the godhouse and took up positions at the head and foot of the sacrificial stone. They were followed by a muscular Indian clad only in a breechclout.

Through the same doorway a prisoner was led forth

206

and placed upon the stone altar, face up. Its curved shape caused his chest to be thrust upward and pulled tight like the skin on a drum.

Two *chacs,* priestly helpers, spread-eagled the young man, holding his arms and legs, though he made no effort to move. The muscular Indian, the *nacom,* swiftly and surely ripped his obsidian knife across the victim's chest. He then reached down into the gaping wound, seized the exposed heart, and snatched it out.

The dwarf said, "It is not new. Centuries past, the Carthaginians sacrificed children to the god Baal-Haman. As many as three hundred in a day were placed upon the outstretched arms of the idol and then rolled off into the fire beneath."

"The acts of ancient barbarians do not condone these acts," I replied.

"The point is, the people of Carthage were not barbarians. Carthage was a city of public baths. We have none. They printed money with marks of value. We use cacao beans. They domesticated animals—hundreds of elephants, for one thing—and used them to carry burdens. We carry burdens upon our backs. Around the city were walls twice as high as those you see before you. Their immense galleys carried goods to a hundred ports from Asia to Britain. The cities they conquered paid them more tribute than ever was paid to Athens. I envision a city that someday we will build together."

The sun went behind a cloud. The gray smoke of St. John the Baptist, the fiery mountain, flowed off into the west. My head reeled. I was silent.

207

∴

I watched in disbelief as the victims were led forth from the godhouse, one after the other, each man painted a bright blue and wearing a peaked, featherless hat. Their blood was caught in a stone basin. There were few sounds from them. Only one young man caused a disturbance. As he was spread out on the curved altar, he raised his head and spat out a series of loud imprecations.

"He is one of Moctezuma's Aztecs," the dwarf said. "They are a rebellious and unrepentant breed. You shall see more of them in the future."

I counted fifteen victims and quit my counting. Through it all, high priest Chalco stood off by himself at the edge of the terrace, silently gazing down upon the throng. Once I caught his eye. He quickly looked away, yet in that brief moment when our gazes met I knew that if it were within his power, he would soon have me stretched upon the sacrificial stone.

As each heart was ripped out, the *nacom* passed it on to a retainer, who rubbed it against a small clay idol. The body was then shoved over the parapet to those below, and the still-beating heart flung after it. A growing hecatomb of hushed hearts lay at the base of the temple, at the very feet of the chanting throng.

"It is an act of devotion," the dwarf said. "Devotion to you. The idol is made in your image."

I had watched the sacrifices with growing disgust, but somehow they were distant, a happening that was not related to me, that would have taken place in memory of me had I not been there.

The murky sky that had cast shifting shadows across the terrace now closed down upon us like a shroud. I tried to speak, to shout my disgust, but managed only a gasping breath.

The *nacom* asked for a new and sharper knife. He was handed a blade of chipped obsidian, carved in the semblance of intertwined serpents. The *chacs* were dripping blood. Their long, black hair was matted with blood. The stone basin overflowed.

Turning in horror, I saw that the great door of the godhouse, through which I had come, was closed and barred. There was no way to reach the labyrinth and disappear. But not three short paces away the terrace ended in midair. I could walk to the edge and launch myself into emptiness. I could leave, in an instant and forever, all that lay around me.

The dwarf must have sensed my thoughts, for he drew closer and put out a restraining hand.

"You and I, we together, will make the city a marvel of the world."

"The city," I said, "is evil. This temple is evil. The mortar that holds it together, stone upon stone, is evilly mixed with men's blood."

The sounds of the chanting crowd grew, then died away, became loud and then clear, until I could hear but one word, Kukulcán. Two of the priests, Hexo and Xipan, were clapping their hands and repeating the word.

The dwarf whispered, "The name that the crowd chants and the priests mumble is not Julián Escobar. It is Kukulcán, Archer of the Skies, Lord of the Dark Arrows, Rider of the Wind of Knives." He paused and stretched out his hands toward the temples and the far sea. "Together we will build a city grander by far than this, grander than Ilium or Carthage. Grander than Rome in the days when Caesar ruled."

As the dwarf whispered these words, a girl not much older than Ceela was placed upon the stone altar and sacrificed. Her heart was flung away. A moment later, she sighed.

There came into my mind at this instant, while the girl's sigh still hung in the air and I realized that she had been sacrificed for me, the scene where Satan took Christ unto an exceeding high mountain and showed Him all the kingdoms of the world and their glory, saying, "All these things I will give thee, if thou will fall down and worship me."

Below, as the girl's heart fell through the air, the multitude was silent.

I heard the voice of Christ. He said, "Get thee hence, Satan."

Chalco was now mumbling my name. I was surprised to hear it from his lips.

The scene on the high mountain, the scene on the parapet—the sacrificial stone, the *nacom* and his bloody attendants, the three high priests—all of it faded. Suddenly there rose before me in a blinding vision the city conjured by Cantú, the dwarf—gleaming temples and spacious ports that sheltered caravels from all the ocean seas, high walls built to withstand every foe, piled goods gained from far-flung trade, treasure wrested from the tyrants of a hundred towns.

The dwarf touched my arm. "Who are you now?" he asked. "Escobar or Kukulcán? Seminarian or Lord of the Shield That Mirrors the Sky, God of the Red House of Dawn?" He tilted his head and glanced up at me. With the same sly calculation I had often noticed, he studied my face. Not waiting for an answer, he answered me: "The seminarian, I can see, is dead."

I could not deny him.

John the Baptist's fiery ring shone brighter now against the mottled sky. The sound of wooden drums, conch shells, trumpets, and many voices grew. From the copal pots that circled the great temple, gray smoke and the smell of sweet incense rose around us. Cantú smiled and did his little dance. The gold ornament he wore around his neck, a serpent coiled and biting itself, glittered even on this sunless day.